LYNCH PARTY!

The mob was coming. They could hear the clatter of boots against the boardwalks, the shouted curses and threats, the whisky-blurred voices blended into an incoherent rumble. Lariats were being brandished aloft and guns banging as men fired into the sky, and Chip knew then that there was very little time if he was to save Sam McAllister. A dim light burned at the front of the jail-building, and the sheriff, swept back by a tide of men, went down under the mob's weight.

Chip had a grip on Sam, but the two of them were surrounded. Somebody shouted, "To the big cottonwood down by Eureka Saloon! That'll make a good hangtree!" The other prisoner had the strength of desperation: the next instant he was running, striking out wildly to the right and left, clearing a lane for himself. The moment he was clear, a dozen guns spoke at once. The convict seemed to leap into the air and half turn around, and he went sprawling in a grotesque heap, his eyes to the sky. Then the mob turned its full attention to Chip and Sam . . .

Also by Norman A. Fox

The Valley of Vanishing Riders

NORMAN A. FOX

A Dell Book

Published by
Dell Publishing
a division of
Bantam Doubleday Dell Publishing Group, Inc.
1540 Broadway
New York, New York 10036

The trademark Dell® is registered in the U.S. Patent and Trademark Office.

ISBN: 0-440-21055-0

Printed in the United States of America

Published simultaneously in Canada

November 1993

10 9 8 7 6 5 4 3 2 1

OPM

Contents

1 : Riders in the Rain

This broken land, this timbered, rocky desolation stretched to the far horizons, a place of emptiness, a place of ponderous silences, a land deceptively peaceful to look upon. From the high ridge where the three waited they could see the whole sweeping panorama of the basin with the cottonwood-fringed creek snaking below them and the scattered brush and rocks and trees all glorious and golden in the last light. Farther away, to the north and west, the high outlines of the Tumblerock Range built a pine-crested barrier, and a storm, gathering about the peaks, painted the sky a muddy hue. Such was the scene, primitive and forlorn, monstrous and eerie, yet somehow magnificent.

To Chip Halliday, possessor of a lively imagination, it was a battlefield for giants, an arena where a Paul Bunyan might have engaged in titanic struggle with some awesome creature of another age. Stretched upon the ridge top, Chip was easing the weariness of his long, lean body, the accumulated weariness of three hard days riding upon a stolen horse, and while he rested, his blue eyes glazed with dreaming, he let his fancy play. Ute Kincade, given to more practical thinking, said, "They're down below, I tell you. I just saw another move in those trees by the creek. They're closing in on us, mister—closing in for the kill!"

Hunkered at Chip's elbow, Kincade now came to a careful stand, moving back from the lip of the ridge. A slack-jawed man who ran to arms and legs, this Kincade had grown more testy each hour that the pursuit had gained upon them. Anger in his little eyes, Kincade said, "Well, are you just gonna lay there, Halliday, till they come and snap the iron on your wrists?"

The third man, old Singin' Sam McAllister, was with the horses, a dozen paces away. A little man with almost half a century of saddle-whacking behind him, his legs were bowed and his egg-shaped head was bald, but he owned a luxuriant yellow moustache of pretentious size. "Lay off the kid," he said. "When he's figured out what to do, he'll tell us. There's more ways of killin' a cat than chokin' it with buttermilk!"

"Sure, keep your shirt on, Ute," Chip drawled. "Remember the bargain when we took you with us? We're running this play, and if you're going to tag along, you've got to do things our way."

"Then let's be doing them!" Kincade snapped. "I'm not going back to Deer Lodge pen, savvy! It's ninety-nine years for me, plus whatever they tack on for making this break. And those boys down below are likely thinkin' of the reward that's been pinned on our scalps!"

Something sang a high, thin song over their heads; a rifle cracked far below; and the silence of the basin was shattered asunder as the walls caught the echo and multiplied it. Kincade shouted, "I saw the smoke! Down there, by that big boulder! Just let him show himself again!"

Dragging a forty-five from a battered holster, he edged forward, but Chip came to a stand then, seizing Kincade's elbow. "Save your lead, you fool!" Chip ordered. "They're out of six-shooter range. You'd just be throwing it away."

"Save your lead!" Kincade babbled. "Save your lead! That's all I've heard since we scaled the wall at Deer Lodge and found these guns at that old empty ranch house that same night. The way you act, Halliday, you'd think those jiggers below were friends. That's Tate Strunk leading that posse, mister! Do you understand? The toughest screw in Deer Lodge pen—a galoot who's a prison guard all the way through—a galoot who's got prison stone and prison steel in his heart and soul. He'll take us back alive, or he'll take us back dead; it makes no never mind to him. And you want me to sit here till he climbs the slope!"

"I want you to use your head!" Chip countered. "Strunk knows our horses are tired; his posse's probably changed mounts a dozen times in the last three days. Likewise he knows he can either starve us out of here or wait till we run low on ammunition. Just don't play into his hands, that's all."

"What are we gonna do?" Kincade wailed.

Old Singin' Sam eyed that spreading darkness above the distant peaks. "Rain's coming," he said.

Down below the rifles were yammering in unison, a score or more of them, and Chip saw now that the posse had spread itself out along the creek. But that thin chain of riflemen was drawing nearer; he marked more than one man darting from bush to stone. And he saw the strategy of Tate Strunk with like clarity; the man was moving up slowly and waiting for darkness to come—the darkness that would cloak the posse while they rushed the slope. These three fugitives had climbed as high as they were going to climb; they had run the legs off their horses, and there was no escape for them. Not unless—

Singin' Sam said, "I've been quiet so long that my vocal chords is likely plumb paralyzed, but I reckon there's no more need to keep hush." Whereupon he began a squeaky and tuneless rendition of a song as old as the Texas trail:

As I walked out one mornin' for pleasure,
I spied a young cowboy a-ridin' alone;
His hat was throwed back and his spurs was a-jinglin',

As he approached me a-singin this song:
Whoopee ti yi yo, git along, little dogies,
It's your misfortune and none of my own,
Whoopee ti yi yo, git along——

"Aw, quit that damn' caterwauling!" Kincade interjected. "This is enough like a funeral without having music throwed in!"

"Rain——!" Sam said exultantly and held out his hand for confirmation.

The gold was gone from the basin now; across the sky the pall of darkness had spread and, below, the shadow had fallen over the land. The drops came, a mere spattering at first, and then hard, driving pellets, lashing down upon these three, making them hunch their shoulders and pull their sombreros low. It was wet and it was miserable up here on this rocky shoulder of a ridge, and there was no shelter for the three. The sky deepened to a scowling black; the light was fast fading; and only the intermittent lightning flashes gave life and shape to the basin below. Beyond the peaks the thunder exploded, and still the guns spoke as before.

"They're getting just as wet as we are," Kincade observed. "But they've likely got slickers—damn 'em. And they'll be comin' now, comin' fast. Another night and we'd have been knockin' at the gates of Forlorn Valley, and once into that land beyond the law, we could 'a' thumbed our noses at every tin-toter in Montana. A fine finish this is!"

Chip, holding silent for many minutes, had been studying the dark pocket of the basin, marking gun-flashes and noticing that they were drawing nearer. Now he said, "Here's where we split up, boys."

"Split up?" Kincade frowned. "What do you mean, Halliday?"

"This darkness can help us as much as it can them," Chip observed. "I'm going down that slope, and I'm taking all three horses with me. And I'm gambling that I'll get chased by the whole bunch; they'll figure we're all making a break for it. That'll leave you two afoot, but it will leave you with a chance to sneak off. It's either that or sit till the bunch climbs up here."

Suspicion narrowed Kincade's little eyes. "You plannin' to get rid of me?" he demanded. "You've wanted to right along. You wouldn't have taken me over the wall with you if I hadn't stumbled onto your little scheme to escape and told you I'd spill the truth to the guards if you didn't cut me in. And now you're gonna shake me!"

Chip sighed wearily. "I'm sick of your company, Ute. I won't lie about that. I'm just as sick of it as I can be. But it happens that you're not being deserted. Singin' Sam will be sticking with you."

"There's something mighty queer about you two," Kincade said. "First place, you only drew three years apiece in stony lonesome, and with good behavior you could have cut that near in half. But with only a month in the pen behind you, you figger a way of getting over the wall—a stunt that's stuck boys who have been inside for years. And once you got out, you were mighty lucky—almost *too* lucky—finding that ranch house with horses and clothes and grub and guns all waiting for us. I tell you, it's mighty funny."

"Haw, haw!" said Singin' Sam with a sour grimace. "I'm laughing at how funny it is, us dodging Tate Strunk's bullets!"

"There isn't time for a lot of useless talk," Chip interjected. "I want light enough so that the posse can see that *three* horses are going down the slope. But I likewise want it dark enough that I'll make a mighty poor target. That's the best scheme I can think up, Kincade. If you're not satisfied, *you* take the ride down the hill, and Singin' Sam and me will fade back into the hills on foot."

"You dreamed it up," Kincade grunted. "You do it."

Chip walked toward the horses; Singin' Sam, a dim blotch in the wet darkness, moved closer to him and thrust out a hand. "Sure this is what you want to do, kid?" the oldster asked.

"It's the only answer; all things considered," Chip said. "You know that, feller. We'll meet in that town called Tumblerock—either there or in Forlorn Valley. Try to keep that prison-locoed killer in line. Failing that, surrender to Strunk or the first lawman you see."

They gripped hands hard, two men who were more than partners in peril, and Chip swung astride one of the horses. Getting a hold on the lead ropes of the other two mounts, he maneuvered so that he had a cayuse on either side of him. Then, giving his sombrero a jerk and bending low over the saddle horn, he prodded his mount with his spurs. "Here goes!" he cried and went over the rim of the ridge and down towards the tilting slope toward the guns that waited below.

Singin' Sam was shouting some sort of farewell, but the wind was in Chip Halliday's ears, and the sound was a blur. Rain had made the slope slippery and thrice perilous, and he went roaring downward, trying to keep at an angle, trying to outflank the posse. The horse to his left stumbled, the lead rope burned through Chip's hand, and the mount went somersaulting. Below, someone shouted, "Here they come!" Thunder exploded and other wild shouts were smothered in that greater sound, but gunflame still blossomed, and Chip felt the tug of a bullet at his sleeve.

He wanted to reach the timber fringing the creek, but to do so he had to break through that ragged line of men who'd moved forward from the creek, and he spurred desperately once he reached the basin's floor. He let the other lead horse go; it went veering away at an angle, and a hoarse voice shouted exultantly: "I spilled one of 'em out of his saddle!"

It was darker than the inside of a pocket, a thick, sloppy darkness, wild with lashing rain, clamorous with exploding thunder. He wondered how it was with the posse, floundering and stumbling through dripping bushes, crawling in the mud and the wet and cursing him and Singin' Sam McAllister and Ute Kincade for giving them such a night's work as this. He reached the brush bordering the creek; branches tore at him, whipped across his face, threatened to wrench him from the saddle. His horse collided with something solid, and the lightning flared then, and Chip had a brief glimpse of the bullet head and piggish eyes of Tate Strunk, the guard whose heart and soul were made of prison stone and prison steel.

Strunk was mounted, and Chip could have shot the man out of his saddle, but instead Chip snatched at the gun he carried and sent a chopping blow at the guard's head. Strunk's own gun was already unleathered, and the man triggered, the darkness blossoming redly, and fire burned along the hard flesh armoring Chip's ribs. For a moment he thought he was going to be torn from his saddle by the slamming impact of the lead, but he got a tight hold on the horn, and he was plunging onward when Strunk's gun spoke again. This second shot came angling upward, and Chip, seeing the flash, knew then that Strunk was upon the ground, felled by his blow. Then Chip reached the creek and splashed into it.

Behind him men were threshing through the dripping bushes, calling and cursing and firing aimlessly, but some, more levelheaded than the rest, were pushing out into the stream, trying to intercept him. He gained the far bank unscathed; he drove through a jungle of bushes, and then he was upon the level floor of the basin again. Giving his horse its head and galloping toward the north, Chip fought against the nausea of his wound.

Now the darkness was more impenetrable than ever, and this rain was washing out any tracks he might be leaving in the rocky ground. He tried doubling and zigzagging, and he crossed the creek twice within the next hour, and he realized then that he'd shaken off any immediate pursuit. But still he forged ahead, not yet convinced that he'd fooled the posse. Perhaps they'd paused to regroup, perhaps they were chasing that riderless horse he'd turned loose at the slope's bottom, or perhaps they'd found their leader stunned upon the ground and were waiting for Strunk to revive before taking up the chase. Chip didn't know.

He had lost all track of time and distance after that. His wound was bleeding and weariness sapped his strength too, but he wasted no moments at trying to fashion a bandage. He was out of the basin within another hour, although he only dimly realized this fact. When lightning flashes gave him glimpses of the Tumblerocks, he fixed his eyes stolidly on those peaks, using them as a landmark and keeping steadily to the north in this fashion. But he knew that this chase was almost over for both him and the horse. There were limits, and Chip had about reached his.

He was a little delirious when he found himself facing the high outline of a gate. Behind the gate loomed a house, a very large house, it seemed to Chip; and he stumbled off his horse and then fumbled with the gate and got it open and lurched inside. Part of him, the part that still held to reality, warned him that he was a fugitive and that to head for this house, or any house, might mean capture and his return to the state penitentiary, but the other part of him, the instinct that cried for rest and warmth and food, sent him onward. He came up hard against something made of stone, and he felt it numbly, felt all around it until his fingers identified the object.

"A well!" He murmured thickly. "A good, old well!"

There was a light in the house, and now another rectangle of orange was etched against the darkness as a door opened, but that rectangle was blurred by something fuzzy and indistinct that blocked it. Chip tried to call out, but the strength wasn't in him. Whoever was coming out of the house was coming toward him, and he put out his hand blindly; and the lightning flared across the heavens then, illuminating the scene with chalky vividness.

Two people had left the house. No, three; for the two were

carrying another between them. The two were slicker-clad, and one was a girl and one was a man; that much Chip was certain about. And the one between them was dead; there was something about the rigidity of him that told Chip the grim truth. He'd been a tall man, this corpse, and he wore a white calfskin vest, and he made quite a load for the two, especially for the girl; Chip could see that.

This much Chip saw and knew, and then the strength deserted him, and a greater blackness, a warm and fuzzy blackness engulfed him, and he ceased to know anything.

2 : **Gun Guardian**

When consciousness came back to Chip Halliday, he found himself in a bed, and at first he was content to just lie there, staring at the ceiling overhead. Rain drummed on the roof that sheltered him, but it was like the tapping of fairy fingers; the back of the storm had been broken, and the muttering thunder sounded vague and distant.

His boots and belt had been removed, he discovered, and likewise his shirt. A bandage pressed against his side where Tate Strunk's bullet had creased him. Letting his eyes rove, he saw that he was in a small room whose furnishings consisted of this bed, a cooking range, a table and some chairs. Flowered curtains at the single window gave the place a feminine touch, and a girl was there, seated at the table with her back to the bed. It was right that a girl should be here, Chip knew, but for a minute he wondered why he had expected one. Then he remembered the two slicker-clad figures toting a corpse between them. A slicker hung on a peg near the door, but there was no sign of the man.

Chip coughed slightly, expecting the sound to bring the girl around with a nervous start. Instead she turned slowly, then came to her feet and crossed over and stood looking down at him. Clad in calico, she had a lithe, supple figure, and her face, oval-shaped and framed by golden hair that fell to her shoulders, was strikingly beautiful. Her blue eyes regarded him calmly, and she added, "So you're awake. I tended to your wound; you'd lost a lot of blood, but you'll heal nicely, I think. I'll spoon some broth into you."

A pot simmered on the cooking range, and she got a bowl from a wall cupboard and filled it with something that steamed and smelled tantalizingly good. When she returned to the bedside, Chip said, "Where am I?"

"In the Bear Creek schoolhouse," she said. "Or rather, in the teacherage attached to the school."

"You're a teacher?"

She nodded. "My name's Hope Brennan. School's out now, but I'm living here through the vacation."

Very solemnly he said, "I'm enrolling, come fall."

She frowned at him. "You're just as fresh as I thought you'd be, Mr. Halliday," she said. "I should have left you out in the rain to cool off. It was quite a job dragging you in and hoisting you to the bed. Already I'm wondering if it was worth it."

So she'd brought him in alone! He wanted to ask her about the man, the one he'd seen her with just before he'd gone unconscious, but his greatest curiosity concerned the fact that she'd called him by name just now. He said, "Was I so delirious that I did some talking?"

"You didn't have to. We see the Great Falls, Helena, and Missoula papers up here in this Tumblerock country," she said. "Those papers have been full of you, and you resemble your pictures, even though you've now got a porcupine prison haircut and need a shave. Where is that reprobate, Singin' Sam McAllister, and that wolf of a Ute Kincade who went over Deer Lodge's wall with you?"

"We parted company," Chip said. She fed him a spoonful of broth, and the warmth of it flowed through him. "Going to turn me over to the law?"

She made no reply, and he said, "You don't like me a-tall, do you?"

She said, "You've quite a record, Chip Halliday, the wastrel son of old Iron Hat Halliday, pioneer stockman who came into this country with the Texas migration and fought Indians and rustlers to build up a spread and a fortune which you'll likely squander the first year after he dies— providing you're not behind bars!"

Propped on one elbow, he grinned at her. "Are you keeping a scrapbook of newspaper clippings about me?" he said.

"People like you interest me," she retorted and spooned more broth into him. "I find it amazing that any one person could have so many opportunities and carelessly kick them out the window. You had a fine schooling in Helena and a free ticket to the university over at Missoula handed to you, Mr. Halliday. Most people I know have to work for those things. You lasted two weeks at the university, according to the papers."

"I wasn't expelled," Chip declared stoutly. "I went out of the dormitory window on a lass rope one night. That was Singin' Sam's fault. Instead of going back to the ranch, he kept hanging around and tellin' me tall tales of elk sign he'd seen up in the Arlee country. The frost was on the pumpkin and nature was a-calling."

"So you quit school, and Iron Hat Halliday chose to overlook that. You came back to the ranch—but not to work. That was too tame for you! So you took to rustling your own father's cattle to pay your gambling and liquor bills."

"I figured those cows would be mine someday anyway," Chip said. "Why wait till I was too old to enjoy 'em? But the old man has quite a temper when he lets go of it, and I guess he reckoned on teaching me a lesson. He shouldn't have jailed Singin' Sam, though. Sam was just out for a moonlight ride the night the sheriff caught up with us. But I'll bet old Iron Hat Halliday's chuckling right now at the way we skinned out of that Deer Lodge pen."

"Likely!" she scoffed. "And you're having yourself a pile of fun, eh? A whooping good game with posses scouring the country for you, excitement in the air and your picture in all the papers. Even getting creased by a bullet hasn't convinced you that you've finally gotten into serious trouble."

"Miss, it's just destiny," Chip declared. "The whole thing was arranged to bring me to your door. That makes up for everything."

His flippancy wrung no smile from her. "Your trail has led steadily northward since you escaped," she said. "That makes it pretty plain that you've been heading for Forlorn Valley. Am I right?"

"They say it's peaceful there."

She studied him with a certain mixture of scorn and calculated appraisal, and she said, "You're almost to the valley. Perhaps I should let you go on in, saying nothing, but I wonder if you know what you're doing. There's one way into Forlorn Valley; there's no way out."

Sagging back against the pillows, he folded his hands meekly. "Tell me about it," he urged.

"Forlorn Valley's been an outlaw hideout for nearly twenty years," she said. "It became a land beyond the law when the remnants of a group of ranchers who'd been on the losing side of a range war herded their cattle to the valley and defied the governor who'd refused them amnesty. Since then other men have come, wanted men from all over the west, men who've vanished from their regular haunts to be seen no more. The man who rules Forlorn gives sanctuary to all those vanishing riders, except killers and renegades of the worst sort. That man is called Clark Rayburn, and the law has no claim on him."

"Then why does he stay in the valley?"

She shrugged. "I don't know; not for sure."

"Did the law ever try to root those men out of Forlorn?"

"It would be impossible," she said. "A few sentries, posted at the right place, could hold off an army. So the law closes its eyes to Forlorn Valley, realizing that those inside are as much in prison as they would be behind bars."

"How do they live?"

"By raising cattle, mostly," she said. "There's room in the valley for twenty times as many people as live there. They graze their cattle, and when marketing time comes, they drive the stuff out of the valley to a ranch that's just this side of the entrance. That ranch belongs to a man named Seton Alessandro, and he buys the cattle from the Forlorners, then sells the beef at a huge profit. Likewise Alessandro provides the valley with the supplies it needs. Also at a profit. Being middleman for the Forlorners is a nice business for Alessandro."

"Alessandro——? Mexican?"

She shook her head. "Half Spanish; half English," she said.

Much of this Chip already knew, but there were also facts he was learning for the first time. Making his voice casual, he said, "Anybody new gone into the valley lately?"

"I wouldn't know," she said. "The point is that whoever goes in, stays in. That's why I'm wondering if you're still determined to enter the valley. You have three years hanging over you if you return to Deer Lodge. You've a lifetime of confinement waiting in Forlorn Valley. The lights aren't very bright in there, Mr. Halliday, and the fun's at a pretty slow tempo. I don't think you'd like Forlorn Valley."

"Perhaps not," he admitted. "But——" Suddenly he stiffened, turned tense by a faint sound in the darkness beyond. At first he'd thought it was the mutter of thunder, but now he knew differently. "Horsemen——!" he shouted. "A lot of 'em! Out yonder in the yard!"

Her eyes darted to the nearer of two doors giving out of this room. "Quick!" she cried. "Can you stand? Get through this door; it will take you into the schoolhouse!"

Kicking aside the blankets, he swung his legs to the floor and came to a stand. For a moment dizziness swept him, and then he was able to take a step. The tattered remnants of his shirt hung on a chair, and his gun and belt and boots were nearby. Snatching up these articles, he heard bit chains jingling, saddle leather creaking as men dismounted.

"My horse!" he cried in stricken remembrance. "They'll find it outside and know I'm here!"

"I led your horse off into the brush and tied him," she cried. "The rain has likely washed out all tracks. Hurry!"

Boots were slogging through the mud of the yard as Hope Brennan flung open the door giving into the schoolroom, and someone pounded imperiously on the other door as Chip eased out of the teacherage, closing the door behind him.

Into a room that was a vast, shadowy pocket, Chip leaned against the wall, fingering his gun. Things had happened too quickly for clear thinking, and he wondered now who rode by midnight and came knocking at this isolated teacherage door. Tate Strunk and his posse? Lawmen from Tumblerock town who'd been warned by telegraph that escaped convicts were near? Cowboys who'd seen a light in the teacherage and come to call? Chip didn't know.

And why had this girl, this Hope Brennan, chosen to shield a fugitive, even going so far as to hide his horse from curious eyes? She had taken him in and tended his wound, too; but he could understand that. He'd probably been no more to her than a stranger in distress when she'd found him facedown in the mud of the yard. Yet once she'd gotten him inside, she'd recognized him from newspaper pictures, but still she'd chosen to shield him. It made a riddle that bewildered Chip. But beyond this door he could now hear the other door creaking open, and the harsh voice of Tate Strunk said in vast astonishment, "It's a gal, fellers. A mighty pretty gal!"

Hope Brennan said coolly, "I don't seem to remember you. Is there something you want, stranger?"

Chip's eyes were growing accustomed to the darkness. He

could make out the precise rows of desks and the larger desk of the teacher, a globe perched upon it. He risked opening the door a fraction of an inch, and thus he got a narrow glimpse of Strunk clawing his sombrero from his bullet head. A thick-shouldered, lumpish sort of man, Strunk was darting his gaze everywhere.

"We're looking for three jiggers who lately escaped from Deer Lodge pen, ma'am," Strunk said. "Anybody come riding this way tonight?"

"In this storm?" Hope said. "I wouldn't have heard them unless they'd ridden right into the yard."

Strunk clapped his sombrero back onto his head, and at this sign of his imminent departure Chip repressed a gusty sigh. But Strunk was looking around again, his little eyes the color of watered milk in the lamplight, and now he said, "That bed! It's all mussed up, ma'am. Yet you ain't undressed, and you didn't have time to dress as we pulled up here. Who was doing some sleeping?"

He came thrusting into the room then, and Chip knew that if Strunk made any sort of examination, he was bound to find some sign of a fugitive's presence. He heard Hope make a slight movement, and his wild thought was that the girl was placing herself in a position to block Strunk. He thought: *If he lays a hand on her, I'm going to have to come out and bend this gun-barrel over his head again, even if it means blowing up the whole fool game!*

He even opened the door wider, and by this means he had a full glimpse of Hope. She wrested open a drawer in the table, and now she had a .38 revolver in her hand, and it was leveled at Strunk's broad chest. She said, "Back up, mister! I see no badge on you, and I'm not having you prowl these premises. You can see for yourself that nobody's here. If you're a real lawman, come back in the morning with Sheriff Busby from Tumblerock, and I'll let you do all the looking you want. And I'll answer all the questions that trouble you. But you're getting out of here now!"

Strunk bared his teeth in a caricature of a smile. "Spunky, huh," he observed. "Now I'm wondering——?"

Outside, someone shouted, "Hey, Strunk! If none of them jailbirds is around, let's go riding. I'd like to find a warm bed somewhere before sunup!"

For an instant Strunk hesitated, and then he said, "Maybe I'm mistaken, ma'am. There'd be no percentage in it for a gal like you to be hiding out a jailbird. But I'll be back tomorrow. With the sheriff. Providing I can find that damn Tumblerock town in this darkness."

"Southwest from here," Hope Brennan said. "More west than south. Good night."

She banged the door shut after Strunk; there was that jingling of bit chains and creaking of saddle leather, the plopping of hoofs in the mud of the yard, and then silence again. After many minutes the girl blew out the lamp and swung open the door leading into the schoolroom.

"I think you're safe, now," she said.

"And grateful," he added, stomping into his boots. "I'll be going now, miss, I don't want any sign of me around when Strunk comes back tomorrow. And he'll come back."

She said, "Still heading to Forlorn Valley?"

"That's the idea."

"You've just said you were grateful," she reminded him. "Now I'm giving you a chance to prove it. You're taking me into Forlorn Valley with you, Halliday, and you're not asking any questions. No, I won't be the excess baggage you think I will. I've figured out the way for us to get into the valley, and I could probably make it alone. But a man might be handy at smoothing the bumps. Is it a deal?"

Nothing that she might have proposed could have startled him more than this, and it took him a long moment to make reply. "I can't do it," he said. "I *am* beholden to you, but I can't do it. From all you told me, Forlorn Valley is a good place to stay out of. What does a girl like you want inside that outlaw hideout?"

"No questions," she reminded him. She still held the .38 revolver in her hand, and she hoisted it and took a steady aim at the teacherage window. "I've no time to waste," she added. "Speak up, or I'll fire; and I'm gambling that the posse is still close enough to hear the gunshot and come roaring back. Is it a deal?"

Once again he remembered the dead man and the two slicker-clad figures carrying it, and it came to him with something of a shock that she might be as much an outlaw as himself, and even more in need of the sanctuary provided by that guarded valley to the north. He grinned ruefully and made his pledge.

"Put down the gun," he said. "It's a deal."

3 : Ruse Gone Wrong

The dawning sun, smiling upon a misty world, warmed a pair of muddied, bedraggled, footsore men who kept to the cover of the high ridges and the brush that dotted this broken land. Ute Kincade and Singin' Sam McAllister had made good their escape from the basin where Tate Strunk's posse had trapped them. With the riders of the law scattered and led astray by Chip Halliday's wild ride down the slope, the other two fugitives had managed to slip away in the darkness and the rain. But this new day found them none too happy with their lot.

Singin' Sam, easing his old carcass down upon a rock, contemplated his worn boots sorrowfully and said, "If I was an octopus, or whatever that critter is that has a hundred feet, I couldn't be more tired. And my stummick's wonderin' who put a padlock on my mouth!"

Hunger and weariness had only served to accentuate the savagery that was Ute Kincade. Sandpapering his stubbled jaw with his fingers, he said, "Halliday played it smart. He kept a cayuse under him and left us pore fools to do the walkin'."

Anger drew some of the slackness out of Singin' Sam, but

he was too tired to voice his loyalty to Chip Halliday. Besides, his eyes had found something unnoticed before, a patch of green, an alfalfa field, likely, that was faintly visible in the more open land below them. "Look!" he cried. "Buildings, beyond that field. A ranch!"

Ute gave his belt a hitch. "Here's where we get some breakfast," he announced and began striding down the slope.

Another time Singin' Sam might have suggested caution, but his own hunger made an insistent demand. He hobbled along after Kincade, trying hard to keep up with the man, and soon they were upon level ground; but the distance to those straggling buildings was greater than it had appeared from above. The two began zigzagging from cover to cover, and the sun stood higher when they reached the alfalfa field. A few horses grazed inside a fenced enclosure, and beyond this there was a small shack with corrals and a stable flanking it. No smoke spiraled from the shack's chimney, and the place had an air of desertion.

Carefully skirting the shack, they found the barn empty. A few half-grown shoats squealed in a pen, and a hen paraded across the yard, leading a brood of chicks behind her. These things spoke of peace and contentment, and Kincade boldly approached the door of the shack, Sam trailing after him, and here they found a note tacked, obviously for the edification of any passing neighbor. It read: GONE TO TUMBLEROCK. BACK LATE TONIGHT.

"Now ain't that just fine," Kincade observed and shouldered into the shack. It was a one-room affair, and of its few crude furnishings, the cooking range won Ute's instant attention. Rummaging around he found bacon and eggs and a full kindling box, and he soon had food on a fire while Sam kept a wary eye at the window.

"Relax," Ute suggested when they sat down at the table. "The only thing we've got to worry about is some other rancher seeing our smoke and dropping in." He tapped his gun significantly. "And that's no worry. Forget about the posse. Either they're still chasing Halliday, or they've turned back to Deer Lodge."

"Not Tate Strunk," Sam said.

"No, he'll cling to the trail as long as there's any sign. But those boys of his have probably got their bellyful by now. A few loiterers from Deer Lodge town who thought the chase might be excitin', a few ranchers who were worried about three jailbirds being on the loose—that's your posse. What have they got to gain by wearing out hosses? Strunk likely held 'em together this far by threats and promises, but they'll be thinking about home after a night like last night."

His meal finished, Kincade leaned back in the chair and propped his feet on the table top with no regard for the crockery. Fashioning a cigarette, he inhaled deeply, a man made contented by food and warmth and a chance to rest his bones.

"We're in luck, Sam," he observed. "Food to pack along—clothes to take the place of these filthy rags we're wearing—hosses waiting to carry us. What more could a man ask?"

Singin' Sam fell to humming, then burst into a snatch of song:

> *It matters not, I've oft been told,*
> *Where the body lies when the heart grows cold;*
> *Yet grant, O grant, this wish to me,*
> *O bury me not on the lone prair-eee. . . .*

"And I've got an idea," Ute Kincade continued. "An idea that'll put me so far away from Deer Lodge that Tate Strunk will never cut sign on me."

"Forlorn Valley?" Sam asked hopefully.

Kincade shook his head. "Last night, with us cornered atop that ridge, I'd have given half an arm to be inside Forlorn Valley. But that was last night. Why should I get holed up in a valley that's the same as a prison? Seattle's where I'm heading. Seattle, where the boats start for Alaska and South

America. But the going will be easier if I get hold of some money."

Pausing, he regarded McAllister speculatively. "The Hallidays are well fixed," Kincade observed. "I'm still thinkin' that escape was mostly engineered from outside the pen, and it takes money to do that. You got any?"

Sam shrugged. "Me, I only worked for Iron Hat Halliday," he said. "And I just tagged along when Chip got hisself in trouble."

"It makes no never mind," Kincade said. "I can get money. We can't be far from Tumblerock town, and I've been remembering something—something that started coming back to me when we headed this way."

Kincade began rummaging around the shack, hauling open drawers, peering into cupboards. At last he palmed a deck of cards with a triumphant grunt. "This is a bachelor's layout," he said. "Figgered he'd have cards to pass away the time at solitaire." Fanning the deck wide, he found the ace of spades, held it aloft for inspection, then tucked it into his shirt pocket. "Here's my ticket to Seattle," he said exultantly. "This little old ace of spades. You don't savvy, huh? Well, it happens that the bank in Tumblerock will cash this card just like it was a check. All I've got to do is write down the amount of dinero I want."

Sam regarded him queerly. "I'm thinkin'," the oldster said slowly, "that they locked you up in solitary about once too often."

Kincade scowled. "I sound loco, eh? Well listen, and I'll spin a yarn for you. Ever hear of the old Grasshopper Gulch diggings?"

"Sure," said Sam. "They had a gold strike down there about twenty years ago. A lot of gents got rich; a lot more broke their backs and their hearts grubbin' in the muck. A town grew up mighty fast, but the ghosts took it over just as fast. I've seen what's left of it—tumbled-down ruins, and rats scurrying across bars that used to bend under the weight of gold dust. What's that got to do with Tumblerock and a bank that cashes aces of spades?"

"There was a lifer in Deer Lodge," Kincade said. "An old hellion called Gopher Joe Gravelly. He died two, three years ago, and I happened to have the next bed to him in the prison hospital when he died. Gopher Joe was down in Grasshopper Gulch at the time of that old strike, savvy. And Gopher Joe watched an all-night poker game that was the kind men never forget. Before dawn that game had narrowed down to two men—a pair of gents who'd been in on the original strike and who owned themselves claims that paid off sweet and often. But one of those gents was the loser and one the winner, and when the sun came up the winner had stripped the loser down to his shirt buttons."

"Easy come; easy go," Sam suggested.

"No; the jigger that had lost everything took it hard; it was a lot more than a night of cards to him; anybody could see that. But there he sat, according to Gopher Joe, with his face looking like a corpse's and only his eyes alive, and then he proposed a last gamble. One cut of the cards, and everything he'd lost might be his again."

"But he was broke," Sam interjected. "What in tarnation did he have to put up?"

"Himself, feller."

"Himself?"

"That was the deal he made. One cut of the cards. If he won, he won everything. If he lost, he belonged to the winner, bone and muscle, heart and soul—his man for life. I tell you, old Gopher Joe took it scary; you could just see that smoky room with the lamp still burning, though the sun was beginning to peek in the window. And those two men making their last play. But the loser lost again. He cut himself a king of hearts, and you could see life coming back into his face. But the other fellow cut an ace of spades and won himself a man."

"Just like that?"

"So far as anybody could see. But Gopher Joe had sharper eyes than most, and he noticed something that escaped the rest of the crowd. The winner drew that ace of spades out of his sleeve before he drew it out of the deck."

"Gopher Joe called his hand."

Kincade shrugged. Gopher was a great gent for mindin' his own business when there was no profit in sight. No, Gopher kept shut; in fact he forgot all about the matter until several years later when his trail happened to take him to Tumblerock. And who should he find but that same gent who'd won a fortune and a man's soul on the turn of a crooked card. Yes, sir, that jigger had left Grasshopper Gulch just after the bubble burst, but he'd left with a sack of money which he'd invested up here. Owned a nice ranch and a town house in Tumblerock—and a bank.

"Things weren't going so well for Gopher Joe then, and he got hisself a big idea. Walking into the bank one day, he slapped down an ace of spades with a hundred dollars written on it, and he said, 'Cash this, feller!' Naturally the cashier just looked at him like Gopher was loco, so Gopher says, 'Don't stand there bug-eyed. If you think this ain't a bonyfide check, just call the big boss of this here money corral.' And in comes the big auger hisself, all neat and decked out, and the cashier spills a fast story. Well, according to Gopher Joe, the boss turned the color of wet putty, but when Gopher said, 'Long time since you cut an ace down in Grasshopper Gulch,' the boss turned to the cashier and said, 'Pay him.'"

Singin' Sam whistled softly.

"After that, whenever Gopher got short, he cashed hisself an ace of spades at the Tumblerock bank. But Gopher was fiddle-footed and he finally blew out of town. Always figgered he'd go back whenever the going got rough, but he was picked up for slow-elking some cows in the Libby country, tried to shoot his way out, and ended up as a lifer in Deer Lodge. And that's the yarn he spun for me while he was coughing out his life. A bank that cashes aces of spades! It worked for him, and it's going to work for me. We're heading for Tumblerock, pronto."

Easing back in his chair, Singin' Sam scratched his bald head, a man visibly impressed. A night-long poker game with a fortune crossing the table. A man made desperate by his losses offering himself as the stake for a last cut of the cards. A palmed ace and an uneasy conscience. A bit of blackmail that had worked for an outlaw now dead. It was fantastic, unbelievable—and therefore likely true. But: "We can't go nosin' into Tumblerock," Sam protested. "Even if Tate Strunk ain't there, the law's likely got word to be on the lookout for two, three strangers lately missin' from stony lonesome."

"That's where you're wrong," Kincade argued. "There's a razor yonder to scrape the fuzz off, and clothes to make us look clean. We'll ride into Tumblerock respectable, and we'll bluff 'em by our boldness. They'll be expectin' us to be out hiding in the bushes, muddy and hungry and crawlin' into our collars at every sound. They'll never dream that we'd tramp their sidewalks like we owned the town. Shucks, man, the easiest place to hide is in a crowd!"

But Singin' Sam shook his head. "It don't make sense to me," he complained.

"It's a thousand bucks in my pocket," Kincade urged. "It's a soft ride on the cushions to Seattle while the law's beating the brush lookin' for us. I'm makin' the try, McAllister, you can trail along, or head a different direction."

It now came to Singin' Sam that he might be standing very close to death. He'd found this Ute Kincade suspicious from the first night when they'd scaled the penitentiary walls, and he knew the man to be cruel and selfish and possessed of all the self-preserving instincts of a ravening wolf. Kincade had chosen to outline this scheme to him, but Kincade would take no chances on entering Tumblerock alone. Not when Singin' Sam might be captured by Strunk meanwhile. Not when Singin' Sam might sing the wrong song and betray the whereabouts of Ute Kincade. A bullet, by Kincade's reasoning, would be a cheap price for silence and security.

Shrugging, Sam said, "Let's take a whirl at it."

A tenseness that had built in Kincade as he'd waited for Sam's answer now eased out of the long-legged man. Grinning, he got the razor, heated water and went to work shaving himself. Sam had his turn with the razor, fought a mental battle as he considered his luxuriant yellow moustache in a cracked mirror, but compromised by merely trimming it. When McAllister finished, Kincade was shrugging into a shirt he'd found among the absent rancher's possessions.

A few minutes later the two were exploring the stable. They found bridles, but only one saddle, a dilapidated hull that had obviously been replaced by a newer saddle which was doubtless now in Tumblerock with its owner. They snaked a pair of speedy-looking saddlers out of the fenced enclosure, and the morning sun looked down upon the pair of them wending toward Tumblerock, Singin' Sam riding bareback.

Both men had a general idea of the direction of the town, and they found a trail of sorts that wound through thinly timbered country and came at last to a road. Doubtless this road led straight to Tumblerock, but the two chose to parallel the twin ruts rather than follow too closely. And this decision was their saving a short while later when a loosely strung cavalcade of horsemen came plodding down out of the north.

Sheltered in a clump of trees, their hands clasped over the nostrils of their horses, Sam and Ute Kincade watched these men ride by. "Strunk's posse," Kincade whispered exultantly. "What did I tell you? They're turning back south. They're all through manhunting."

"But Strunk's not with them," Sam observed.

This near brush with the law made them even more wary as they resumed their riding, but they saw no other riders in the ensuing hour, and the end of that hour brought them to Tumblerock. A brawling creek skirted the town, possibly the same creek that cut through the basin where they'd been trapped the night before, and a wooden bridge, spanning this creek, led into the main street of the town, a straggly row of false fronts made leafy by a profusion of trees that lined the way. Before they reached the bridge, Sam called for a consultation. A range veteran, he realized that the horses they rode themselves might be more of an object of attention than themselves, and, since the owner of these horses was in Tumblerock, recognition might mean disaster.

"But we'll be even more noticeable if we come in afoot," Kincade protested.

They compromised by deciding to ride into town but to dismount as soon as it was feasible, and they rumbled over the wooden bridge and swung from the horses almost at once. Sam spied a line of saddlers tied in a shadowy slot between two buildings, and they led the mounts back among these other horses.

Then the two went clumping up the boardwalk, Sam fighting an urge to tug his floppy sombrero low, while Kincade, following his strategy of bluff, walked boldly with his head thrown back. This Tumblerock was a fair-sized town, the trading center likely for a vast area of mountains and range, and the main street bustled with people who all seemed bent upon business of their own. No man challenged them, no one gave them more than a casual glance; and they came past a livery stable, a blacksmith's shop, a millinery store, and, at last, to the bank.

"Now!" Kincade said softly. "Stay at my elbow and keep your eyes peeled. I'll do the talking."

The bank was a two-storied structure, made of red brick that had grown rusty through the years. A big bay window fronted it, and a name was emblazoned in gold letters upon the window. Inside, the two crossed a big room, their bootheels echoing hollowly against a wooden floor, and Kin-

cade headed for a cashier's grilled window that had no loiterers about it. He'd scratched his four-figure needs upon
that ace of spades before they'd left the deserted ranch, and
now he slipped the card under the grille and said, "Like to
get this cashed, please."

The cashier, a pasty-faced youngster with black hair plas-
tered thinly against a high skull, stared in astonishment.

"You don't savvy?" Kincade queried with an affable grin.
"Take this card to your big boss and ask him if it ain't OK.
Him and me have a little special arrangement about such
matters."

With a puzzled frown, the cashier backed out of his cage,
leaving the card lying. Kincade picked it up, and a great
feeling of uneasiness began to build within Singin' Sam
McAllister as the minutes marched while they waited. The
bank was quiet, deathly quiet; men made small talk at the
counters and windows, a fly buzzed disconsolately in and out
of the open door.

Three things had brought Singin' Sam to Tumblerock; one
was the fear that to refuse might have precipitated a gun-
fight, a second was the fact that Chip Halliday had mentioned meeting him here, the third was a great curiosity to
see whether Ute Kincade's fantastic story had any founda-
tion in fact. But Singin' Sam was already regretting this
thrusting of their heads into what might be a trap, and each
passing minute sharpened that regret.

Then the cashier reappeared. He came through that open
front doorway, and Sam realized then that an unseen back
door must have let the fellow out of the bank. With him
were two men, one short and rotund and gray, the other big
and dark and burly with a sheriff's star pinned to his vest.
The one with the badge had a forty-five in his hand, and the
cashier pointed and said shrilly, "There they are! Those two
by my window!"

Singin' Sam heard Ute Kincade's low curse, then he could
almost feel the man stiffen. He wondered then, did Sam, if

Kincade would try for his gun, turning this bank into a roaring bedlam of thunder and flame and death in another instant. But Kincade's nerve went ebbing and Kincade's hands hoisted, and Singin' Sam raised his own arms.

"You've nailed us, sheriff," Sam said. "Easy on that trigger."

The sheriff peered. "And a good day's work it is," he said. "I thought I was catching me a pair of holdup men with a new wrinkle. It seems I've bagged a couple of flown jailbirds. You shore do fit the description."

"You can't arrest me!" Kincade cried desperately. "Where's Seton Alessandro? Ain't he still the big boss of this bank? You'd better let me have a word with him!"

"You'll have a word with nobody," the sheriff countered. "You're marching down to the hoosegow!"

To Singin' Sam there came the memory of an old song that had to do with jails and bars and a prisoner's weary plaint. But there was no heart in him now for singing.

4 : The House of Alessandro

On a high crest of land overlooking Tumblerock sat the town house of Seton Alessandro, a sprawling edifice of no coherent design, a structure of many windows and many gables, expressive of the whims of a much-traveled man who had looked upon dwellings in the far corners of the earth and incorporated the memory of them into this place he called home. It was fascinating, yet repellent. It was magnificent and arrogant and domineering. It was Seton Alessandro expressed in frame and stone.

To reach this house, one followed a twisting trail that coiled upward from the western end of Tumblerock's main street, and thus those who came to call upon Seton Alessandro climbed upward to his abode and were in this manner reminded of their own inferiority. And under the hot nooning sun, Jasper Fogg, attorney at law, made the ascent.

A short, rotund gray man, this same Jasper Fogg had been with the sheriff when Singin' Sam McAllister and Ute Kincade had been trapped in the bank. A man of many accomplishments, Fogg was not, however, adept at anything calling for physical prowess. He could draw up a brief that was perfection down to the last comma; he could make a Fourth

of July oration that tingled the toenails of his listeners; but
he had left some part of him in the bottoms of each of the
thousand whisky bottles he had emptied.

Puffing and blowing when he reached the shade of the
great portico, he paused to mop his round, pink face. He
wore a black suit that was baggy and shapeless; his string tie
was all askew, and he said aloud, "That's part of his damn
psychology, blast him! He makes sure that no man could
look his best after climbing that goat's trail to reach him!"

Hoisting the iron knocker, he gave it a resounding clang.
A moment later a buzzer hissed waspishly, releasing the
door lock, and Fogg started nervously as he always did at
this newest innovation of Alessandro's. He put his hand to
the door and stepped into a high, arched hallway, the polished floors giving back the echo of his shuffling boots as he
followed the hall to the study of Seton Alessandro.

It was a lavish room, this study, high-ceilinged and well
lighted and with a yawning fireplace against one wall.
Mounted animal skins, toothy-headed and glassy-eyed, made
rugs for the floor—lions and tigers and a grizzly bear—while
over the fireplace hung a pair of crossed elephant tusks and
an Ashanti spear, tokens of Alessandro's prowess as a
hunter, testimonials of the extent of his travels. A gun case
ran the width of one far wall, and its contents would have
gladdened a connoisseur's eye. And behind a handsomely
carved teakwood desk, in the center of all this exotic splen-
dor, sat Seton Alessandro.

"Good morning, Jasper," he said.

A tall man, Alessandro had a figure kept lithe and active
by constant exercise with the foils. But it was his face that
always compelled attention. There was something of the
scholar in his high sweep of forehead, something of the cynic
in his thin lips and narrow nose. He had an olive tinge to his
flawless complexion, and his velvety eyes also spoke of the
Latin half of his blood. In another setting, he would have
been the perfect Spanish grandee, hearty master of some

vast land grant from a distant and careless king. Yet a black robe and flickering candlelight would have fitted him into a picture of Torquemada's council, sitting in sadistic session in medieval darkness.

Today Alessandro wore a suit of black velvet, designed for riding. His polished boots reflected the sunlight, his coat fitted him snugly across the shoulders, and he looked so cool and self-contained that the sight of him whetted the irritation of Jasper Fogg. It was with studied intent, then, that the lawyer did not instantly broach the reason for his visit.

"I was up here last night," Fogg said. "The lights were burning, but nobody answered the door."

"I rode out to the ranch just before the storm," Alessandro said, and waved Fogg to a high-backed chair. "The hounds are getting fat and lazy from lack of exercise. Do you suppose there's still another grizzly to be flushed out of the Tumblerocks?"

"I don't know," Fogg snapped waspishly and eyed the wine decanter on Alessandro's desk. "Sheriff Busby's not complaining for lack of the kind of game he hunts. He bagged two of those escaped convicts this morning."

Alessandro's interest was a study in bored politeness. "That should make Frank very happy," he said.

"He's had an empty jail for quite a while," Fogg observed. "Now he has a pair of important prisoners. There was a posse in town from Deer Lodge early this morning, but they'd given up the hunt. They all headed south except the man who was leading them. He's a prison guard named Strunk. I think your hounds could take lessons from him, Seton. Only Strunk's strain runs more to bulldog from the look of him."

"Busby turning the prisoners over to him?"

"Strunk's gone. Left his own horse at the livery, rented a fresh cayuse and lit out again before the capture."

Alessandro's boredom was beginning to show in a certain

restlessness that ran through him. "Frank shouldn't need any advice in a case of this kind," he said.

"I'm not so sure," Fogg countered. "I'm the one who was responsible for the arrest. One of the bank cashiers came bustling over to my office less than half an hour ago. The youngster was all excited, claiming a couple of suspicious-looking gents had come to his window. When he told me about the matter, I took him to the sheriff. We bagged the pair of them without a gunshot."

"Then you and Frank split the glory," Alessandro said and yawned. "There should be enough to go around."

"Oh, sure," Fogg agreed. Then: "Those fellows were trying to cash an ace of spades, Seton."

He jarred Alessandro with that; he could see it in the way the man stiffened, and Fogg's unholy delight almost expressed itself in a smile.

"An ace of spades!" Alessandro echoed. "You mean they were trying a bit of blackmail?"

"That seemed to be the idea."

"Have they talked since they were arrested?"

"The old coot, Sam McAllister, has been doing some singing since he got put in a cell, but not the kind to worry you, Seton. The other one, Ute Kincade, wanted a word with you at first. But he's stayed sullen and silent since then."

"There were three," Alessandro said. "I've been following the account in the papers. What about the other—that young Halliday kid?"

Fogg shrugged. "He wasn't with them."

Alessandro frowned darkly and began drumming on the desktop with his fingertips, a nervous, thoughtful tattoo. "There was that other fellow, several years ago," he said. "What was his name? Gopher Joe Gravelly. I should have put a bullet into him, but I bought him off instead. He drifted away just about the time I'd decided to quit humoring him. But he died in Deer Lodge; we know that. And now there's another flashing aces of spades around."

"The answer is obviously simple," Fogg observed. "Gravelly and Ute Kincade were in the pen at the same time. Gravelly doubtless told Kincade about his little blackmailing business. Kincade, free and finding himself in the Tumblerock country, thought he'd try his hand at it."

"But if Kincade knows, how many others did Gravelly tell as well?"

Fogg hoisted his shoulders again. "Probably no one. It's not the kind of secret a man sows to the four winds."

Alessandro came out of his chair and began a nervous crossing and recrossing of the room. "Now this!" he exclaimed explosively. "Why do troubles have to gather all at once? Look at that situation in Forlorn Valley. Clark Rayburn's getting harder to manage every day, and it's all I can do to keep him from kicking over the traces. We've got a sweet thing there, Fogg; doing business for the Forlorners bags us money coming and going. But I tell you it won't work if Rayburn doesn't manage things inside the valley. And now this jailbird shows up, flashing cards and trying to shoot off his mouth. I tell you, Fogg, I have a feeling that the walls are beginning to totter all around me!"

"You'll find a way to bolster them up," Fogg said placidly.

Alessandro ceased his restless pacing and fixed a hard and penetrating stare upon Jasper Fogg. "Yes," Alessandro said. "I'll find a way. As you leave, call Colorado Jack Ives and send him to me. He's probably down at the stable."

Thus curtly dismissed, Jasper Fogg shuffled out of the room, casting one last longing look at the wine decanter but winning no nod of approval from Alessandro. The lawyer gone, Alessandro seated himself at the desk once more, placed his fingertips together above the polished surface and fell to thinking, his velvety eyes far away and fathomless. He was like this when a catlike tread aroused him many minutes later, and he looked up to see a broad-shouldered man in range garb standing in the doorway.

"Oh, come in, Colorado," he invited. "I've got a job for you."

This Colorado Jack Ives was one of those men who are ageless. Good-looking in a weathered sort of way, he wore a close-clipped moustache, and when he thumbed back his sombrero, he revealed a feather of gray along the edge of his blue-black hair. A man unschooled in the hiding of his emotions, he frowned darkly as he advanced to seat himself. Tipping the wine decanter, he sloshed a glass full and downed it. "Well, what is it now?" he demanded.

Alessandro studied him reflectively before speaking. Then, without prelude, he said, "Frank Busby jailed two of those escaped convicts today. Singin' Sam McAllister and Ute Kincade. A prison guard named Tate Strunk is roaming the hills and will doubtless be back soon to claim those prisoners. Before Strunk gets here, I want the two of them lynched."

Colorado Jack snapped his fingers. "Just like that, eh?"

"You know how to arrange it," Alessandro said. "A little free liquor at the saloons. A little talk about what a pair of murderous skunks they are. You can prepare yourself by reading the newspaper accounts, if you like. Ute Kincade was serving a life sentence for murder, as I remember it. He's got a hanging coming to him. McAllister is another story; he appears to be an old fool who let his boss's kid lead him into trouble. But once you've got a mob worked up, they won't take time to separate the gray from the black. It's Kincade I want dangling, Colorado. But McAllister happens to know what Kincade knows, I'd guess, so he's got to die too."

Ives came to a stand, his mouth drawn tight and straight. "And what would you say if I told you I won't do it?"

Alessandro smiled. "You're getting hard to manage too, Jack," he said. "Can it be that the foremanship of my ranch has lost its appeal for you? Am I to presume that you'd rather be in Forlorn Valley than enjoying the comparative freedom that I allow you?"

Ives said, "OK. You've got me pinned to a card, and you'd like to see me squirming. You won't, mister. But here's a thought for you to grab on to. Maybe someday there'll be one job that will be just a little bit too strong for my stomach."

"But it won't be this one," Alessandro softly mocked. "You'd better get along, Colorado. Twilight is the hour for lynching; it will take you all afternoon to stir up a mob. Hurry now. I don't want this Strunk showing back to claim his prisoners and spoil the game. Behind bars, Kincade can still talk, and other men will be leaving Deer Lodge in the days to come—through the gate and over the wall. Ah, but you don't understand what I'm talking about."

"I understand what you want," Ives said and, turning on his heel, he strode from the room.

He came down the hallway toward the front door with anger riding him, but somewhere in the shadows he felt a soft, arresting hand upon his arm. "Jack!" a voice whispered, and he let himself be drawn into a carpeted room.

"Lia," he said softly and all of his anger ran out of him.

Lia Alessandro was small and she was dark, and in this shadowy room of drawn shades she made a petite figure in jodhpurs and a white silken shirt. Sometimes Colorado Jack Ives reminded himself that she was akin to those mounted animal hides and those elephant tusks and the other trappings of this house that spoke of distant climes. But now, as always when he could feel the closeness of her, the warmth of her, he had to put a practiced restraint against his need to sweep her into his arms.

"You have not come to see me for many days, Jack," she said. "You were going to leave the house now without seeing me. Have I angered you?"

He said hoarsely, "Angered me? I've walked nights, trying to drive you from my mind. It's no use, Lia. It's as hopeless as the mountain loving the moon. Even if there was nothing else to stand between us, *he'd* keep us apart."

"Are you so sure, Jack? Let me talk to him. Let me tell him about us."

He shook his head. "I know him," he said. "I know him too well for that." He looked at her long and thoughtfully. "What are you to him, Lia?" he demanded. "That's one thing I'll never be able to savvy."

Her shrug might have been Latin, might have been Oriental, or perhaps a mannerism unconsciously copied from the master of this house. "All my life I've lived here, or at the ranch, except when I've been away to school," she said. "All my life I've been Lia Alessandro. Sometimes he says he is my uncle; sometimes he just laughs when I ask him. I do not know."

In a strained voice, he said, "Has he—has he ever . . ." She understood the fear he dared not speak, and she said, "No, Jack. Only as a father loves a daughter. But sometimes he scares me; sometimes there are things I cannot understand. But he has been kind to me, Jack; he has given me a home and food and schooling."

"He's cruel," Ives said. "Cat cruel. He uses men as some riders use a horse, to serve at the moment and to be left when there's no longer any need. Look at Fogg. Fogg hates him; I can see it in the old devil's eyes, yet Fogg comes running whenever Seton barks. And there's me and Clark Rayburn, and all of the men in Forlorn Valley, for that matter. Chessmen for him to move about as he pleases."

Lia said, "We could run away . . . far, far away . . ."

"And live with his shadow hanging over us all the time," Ives countered. "No, Lia; it wouldn't work. And I've got to be going now, to do another chore for him. He's probably listening for the front door to open and shut. He's maybe even hearing what we're saying to each other. This house is *him,* I tell you; its ears are his ears."

He moved toward the door, but she caught at his arm again, clinging tightly. "You'll come to see me?" she begged.

"I'll come," he promised. "I'll come even when I'm trying to stay away."

Then he was out of the room and to the door leading from the house, a man recalled to reality and bent upon grim business of another man's willing.

5 : To Tumblerock

The same dawning sun that had looked upon Ute Kincade and Singin' Sam McAllister as the two had toiled toward the deserted ranch also smiled upon Chip Halliday and Hope Brennan, who were covering the miles in an easier fashion.

They'd left the schoolhouse in the darkness before dawn, this pair, Chip riding his own horse which the girl had staked out in the brush, while Hope was now astride a saddler she'd kept in a lean-to adjacent to the teacherage. She had traded calico for a pair of jeans, faded from many tubbings, and a plaid flannel shirt, and in this rougher garb and with her long golden hair tucked under a sombrero, she looked like a lithe, handsome boy.

It was she who pointed the way, and their trail took them through screening timber, buck brush slapping against their legs as they rode single file. In this tumbled country they seemed to be always climbing, and at last they came out upon a promontory overlooking a wide, green hollow dotted intermittently with parklike glades. It was such a scene as Chip had looked upon from the rocky ridge where Tate Strunk had trapped the fugitives last night, only this was a broader basin, its level floor stretching far away until it merged with the shadowy blue of evergreens which, in turn, climbed to blend into the misty purple of the mountains. Surveying this wild panorama thoughtfully, Chip glanced at the girl. "Forlorn Valley——?" he asked.

She shook her head. "They call this Bear Creek Basin," she said and pointed northward. "See where it pinches together? That's the narrow pass leading into Forlorn. And that's our stumbling block, for Clark Rayburn keeps sentries posted constantly at that pass."

Nearer and toward the south end of this basin, Chip now vaguely perceived a scattering of buildings almost lost from view in a clump of trees. "A ranch——?" he wondered aloud.

"Seton Alessandro's place," Hope exclaimed. "Sometimes the men of Forlorn venture this far south, to bring their cattle to Alessandro for sale. In a sense Alessandro guards the gate to Forlorn Valley. Alessandro plays well within the law, but you can be sure he'd stop anybody who he thought had no proper business inside Forlorn."

Something in her remark aroused his quick interest. "You mean that Alessandro might know of anybody else who's tried to get inside Forlorn lately? Might even have stopped that someone?"

His intensity betrayed him. Giving him a sidelong look, Hope said, "Last night you asked if anybody had gone into the valley recently. Is there someone you are hunting?"

He had to smile at her quickness of perception. "We made a deal," he reminded her. "I was to ask no questions of you. I'm claiming the same exemption."

She shrugged. "It doesn't matter. We both want to get into the valley, and I told you I knew a way."

"I'm listening," he said.

"As I mentioned before, Alessandro furnishes the Forlorners with supplies—at a high profit," she said. "Those supplies are freighted in by bullwhackers working for Alessandro. Naturally the sentries at the pass let the bullwhackers enter. If my calculations are right, wagons may be going through today. My plan is to sneak ourselves aboard one of those wagons, somehow, and take a chance that they won't be examined too closely at the pass."

"What about these horses?"

"They've fetched us here and saved us a mighty long walk," Hope pointed out. "We'll still need them if it happens we have to wait here two or three days before freighters come through. This way we'll be able to sneak back to the schoolhouse by night for more grub, if we need it. Once the freighters show up, we can always cache the saddles and gear and turn these cayuses loose to forage for themselves."

He raised his eyebrows in applause and considered this golden girl with a growing respect. She had proved herself cool in the emergency of Tate Strunk's arrival last night. Afterward she had showed a hard head in driving her bargain with him, Chip Halliday. And now she'd displayed a generalship that took everything into account. He said, "You don't really need me, you know. I suspect you could get into Forlorn Valley or anywhere else you were minded, all by your lonesome. Thanks for taking me along."

"We're not there yet," she reminded him. "And we've probably got a long wait. We might as well settle ourselves comfortably."

Hobbling the horses, they stripped the gear from them and spread the saddle blankets in the scanty shade of a lodgepole pine. From this vantage point they could keep an eye on the basin below them, but Chip, weary and weak from the night before, dozed away, his head pillowed on his saddle, and at high noon was awakened by the light touch of the girl's hand upon his shoulder.

"Company coming?" he asked sleepily.

"Not yet," she said. "I thought you might be hungry. In any case, it may be a long time between meals if we do manage to hide ourselves aboard a wagon."

He said, "Do you know, I like being with you. I don't even have to think. Will you marry me?"

"I'm not interested," she said: "That surprises you greatly, I suppose. You're sure that any girl in the world would jump at the chance. But the man I marry has to have some sense of responsibility and both feet planted squarely on the ground. Chip, tell me, seriously, can you imagine a more undependable prospect than being married to you?"

He grinned broadly. "You'd feel different if I was shaved and prettied up," he said.

"Here!" she said and thrust food at him.

Munching this cold food she'd stuffed into a saddle bag before they'd left the teacherage, he studied the basin below him. No riders showed themselves around Alessandro's ranch, no smoke lifted above the treetops, and these signs of desertion interested him. But with the food eaten, he grew sleepy again, and once more he dozed upon the blanket. Sometimes he dreamed, and his dreams were a tangle of people and places, with Singin' Sam and Ute Kincade and Tate Strunk and Hope Brennan stalking through them. And once again he was aroused by the girl's touch upon his shoulder.

"You mutter in your sleep," she said. "That's another reason I wouldn't marry you. But look!"

He saw now that the sun was veering toward the west; the afternoon was almost gone and he was surprised that he'd slept so long. But it was the objects the girl indicated that really riveted his attention. Snaking across the basin floor and skirting a flashing creek that meandered out of the north came four high-sided freight wagons in single file, six-yoke of oxen hitched to each wagon while the bullwhackers strode along, the popping of their whips reaching Chip faintly at this far distance.

"That's them, sure enough," he said. "What now?"

"We'll leave our horses here and go down on foot," she said. "Our big job will be to get aboard a wagon undetected, and we'll have to leave that to chance. If we make it, fine. If not, we can come back to our horses; even unhobbled they won't be strayed too far away."

He gave her a stiff military salute. "Yes, sir. As you say, sir," he said.

She smiled. "Come on," she urged.

The horses unhobbled and left behind, they went walking down into the basin, keeping low and maneuvering from one clump of trees to another. They moved at an angle, their object to intercept the slow-moving wagons. But as the distance narrowed, Chip began to regard Hope's plan with growing misgivings. How could they manage to get aboard a wagon without being seen by the bullwhackers?

The freighters had vanished into a grove of trees; now the wagons reappeared, but there were only three of them. No more than a quarter of a mile separated Chip and the girl from the timber that hid the missing wagon, and the two went forward at a hard run, bending low and bobbing into the leafy shelter. They could make out the fourth wagon ahead of them, the canvas top glimmering whitely through the interlacing branches where it stood unmoving and as they wormed as close as they dared, a bullwhacker came stomping back along the trail.

"Pete," the fellow demanded. "What in blazes is holding you up?"

"My front axle's been crying for grease ever since we left Tumblerock," Pete replied. "I've got to do some daubing now, or I'll never make it over the pass."

Crawling closer, Chip could see both bullwhackers, a pair of big, thick-chested men wearing the broad-brimmed hats, flannel shirts and pants tucked into high-legged boots that was the usual garb of their breed. The one who'd come back mopped his forehead with a large bandanna and said, "A hot day and a dull job, Pete. I wish we was back in town. At least there's free liquor and excitement there."

"And a lynching by the time it gets deep dark," Pete said.

"It was shore getting off to a proper start, if I ever saw the sign. Did you see them two prisoners? The Kincade looks like he needs a hanging, they say, but McAllister seemed to stack up as a kindly old galoot."

Chip had his hand on Hope's arm, and his fingers bit deeply. He began wriggling backwards, still keeping as quiet as possible, and the girl, frowning in puzzlement, could do nothing but follow him. When they'd withdrawn to a safe distance, she whispered, "What's the matter with you? We had a perfect chance there. While he was under the wagon doing his greasing, we might have been able to slip inside!"

Chip said, "We've got to get back to the horses! And we've got to get to Tumblerock by the shortest trail!"

She said, "I don't understand——?"

"I'm not sure I do either. But Ute Kincade and Singin' Sam McAllister are in jail in Tumblerock. Didn't you hear what that bullwhacker said? And the town's fixing to lynch them sometime tonight!"

Hope said, "We made a deal. You were to take me into Forlorn with you. Sheriff Busby will stop that lynching."

"Our deal still goes," he said fiercely. "But Forlorn Valley can wait. There's nothing in this world that matters much to me with Singin' Sam in danger. And I'm not depending on any badge-toter to get him out."

All the levity had left him, all his easygoing ways were discarded as a coat is shed. He was a man possessed of one gnawing need, and one only, and a look at him was enough to know that he'd brook no interference, be swayed by no argument. They went back across the basin floor, making little effort at keeping to cover, and they toiled up the hillside to the same clump of lodgepole pine where they'd hidden the saddles and gear.

Now they had to thresh through the timber, searching for the horses they'd turned loose, and Chip was in a frenzy of impatience until he found the two, not far away, and settled a noose over their necks. When he was mounted a few minutes later, Chip looked to Hope. "Point the way to Tumble-rock," he said. "The fastest way."

She nodded and headed her horse southwest, skirting the rim of the basin and coming down onto the broad floor somewhere below Alessandro's ranch. They rode at a brisk gallop, but there were places where the trail forced them to walk. It was in one of these stretches that Chip began speaking, softly and almost to himself.

"Sam McAllister worked for my father before I was born," he said. "My mother died when I was button-size, and Singin' Sam was mother, partner and teacher to me. It was him put me aboard my first cow pony. It was him untangled my twine when I learnt to rope. He taught me to cuss and to chew tobacco, but he also taught me to give the other fellow an even shake. He got me into trouble time and again, but mostly it was the other way around, him following wherever I led. A lot of the gray in Iron Hat Halliday's hair comes from schemes the two of us dreamed up, yet in all the years I never found any real wrong in Singin' Sam McAllister."

Hope said, "I'm sorry. I didn't quite understand—until now."

His eyes mirrored a fierce determination. "If we get to Tumblerock too late, I'll tear down that town, stick for stick and stone for stone. Do you understand me? I'll root out every man that has a hand in the lynching, even if I have to chase them from here to Mexico!"

But they didn't come to Tumblerock too late. They rode in as gray dusk swept from the hills and the town lay murky and shapeless under that mantle. They clattered across the wooden bridge that came up the main street, finding it uproarious with life, the saloons blazing brightly and all of them echoing the throaty rumble of liquored men who were working themselves to the proper pitch for the kill. The sign was here, plain to see, plain to read. The fury was gathering; soon it would unleash itself. There weren't many minutes to spare.

Up until now Chip had formulated no plan, considered nothing but the desperate need to reach this town in time. He had forgotten that he himself might be risking the same fate that threatened Singin' Sam and Ute Kincade by coming here. He had forgotten that it would take more than his mere arrival to stave off a mob. But caution came to him again, and he pulled his lathered, blowing horse in to a hitchrail and stepped down from the saddle.

"Where's the jail?" he asked Hope.

"Up there," she said and pointed to the far end of the street where a structure of frame and stone loomed dimly.

He said, "I'm mighty grateful to you for pointing the trail. I might have lost hours just trying to locate this town. But you'd better fade now; it wouldn't do for you to be seen with me. Head for the teacherage and wait there. If I get through safely, I'll join you as soon as possible. And we'll take another try at Forlorn Valley then."

"I'll hang around a while," she said. "I'd like to see this thing through."

He frowned, trying to muster an argument that would sway her from such a purpose, but he knew he had no time to waste in arguing. Turning, he headed toward the jail-building, and though he didn't look back, he had the feeling that she was swinging from her saddle. Along the boardwalk he strode, shouldering against the steady stream of men that flowed restlessly. Now he could see the high rise of land at the western end of the street and the big, lighted house that perched upon it, but the building had no interest for him. Soon he reached the shadowy region of the jail, and here he paused, listening intently as a snatch of song floated from one barred window:

> Cloudy in the west, and it looks like rain,
> And my danged old slicker's in the wagon again,
> Come a ki-yi, yippy, yippy yi, yippy ya,
> Come a ki-yi, yippy, yippy ya-a-a-a . . .

"Sam!" Chip said softly and smiled.

He knew now which cell held the oldster. To the west of the jail-building was a weedy lot, and he moved off into the shadows that thronged it, moved stealthily toward the window from which the song had come. And here it was that he found a man loitering, a lumpish man who bulked out of the night.

"Howdy, Halliday," said the man. "It's been a long wait, but I had a hunch that Singin' Sam McAllister would be the proper bait to bring you to me. Now get those hands up!"

And the first starlight glinted faintly on the gun that prison guard Tate Strunk held in a steady hand.

6 ⋮ Blood on the Ace of Spades

Stiffening with the shock of surprise, Chip instinctively raised his hands shoulder high. When he'd calculated the many dangers he might meet in Tumblerock, he'd not expected Tate Strunk to be here, at least not hunkering in the shadows in such a manner as this. Strunk's place was with the prisoners, and because, by the guard's own admission, Strunk had been hiding here instead of contriving to remove Singin' Sam and Ute Kincade beyond the mob's reach, Chip said, "Just what kind of cards are you playing, Strunk?"

The prison guard took a step nearer. "I rode a wide circle today and came back to Tumblerock to find two of my birds caged," he said. "But it was the third that interested me. I kept shut and took a stand here. Now it's paid off."

A heady anger put an edge to Chip's voice. "You mean you've made no move to get Sam and Ute out of this town?" he demanded. "Man, don't you savvy that a mob's liquoring for a kill?"

"So you know that?" Strunk said. "And you want no harm to come to Singin' Sam's old carcass? I can claim the prisoners and have them on the way to Deer Lodge inside half an hour, Halliday. But first I'd like a little talk with you. And I'll just hoist that gun out of your holster."

Down the street the many-voiced mutter of the mob had converged into one chaotic roar. Singin' Sam had ceased his singing; whether the oldster had heard voices beyond his cell window and was now crowded up against the bars listening, Chip couldn't tell. In the comparative hush of this remote end of the street, Strunk took another step nearer, reaching with his left hand for the gun at Chip's thigh. And at that same moment there was a slight sound off in the darkness—something that might have been the crunching of a boot sole against a pebble. Instinctively Strunk turned his head, his eyes questing the shadows, and that single, unguarded moment was all that Chip needed.

His hands dropping, he sent his left fist lashing at Strunk's jaw, and as he struck Chip pivoted on his heel, putting all his weight behind the blow. Chip's knuckles sledging against Strunk's blunt chin, the prison guard went down, his gun roaring at the sky, and instantly Chip was upon him, wrenching the gun away and flinging it aside. Expecting to have a fight on his hands, Chip was astonished to find Strunk limp beneath him, and it was a moment before he understood. Strunk's head had struck against a rock as the man had fallen, and the blow had taken the consciousness out of him.

Another form loomed out of the shadows, and Hope Brennan's voice came cautiously, whispering, "Chip——?" And Chip knew then who'd made that slight sound that had drawn Strunk's attention.

Singin' Sam was whispering too, from the jail window. He said, "Good work, Chip! Heard you two palavering out there and recognized the voices. I was just hoping that Strunk would get close enough to these bars so that I could peel off a boot and bend it over his thick skull."

Hope, peering down at Strunk's sprawled, bulky form, said, "Why it's that man who came looking for you at the teacherage last night! Is he——?"

"Not dead," Chip said. "Just stunned. Maybe we'd better get him roped and gagged before he wakes up."

"Listen!" Hope cried.

The mob was coming. They could hear the clatter of boots against the boardwalks, the shouted curses and threats, the whisky-blurred voices blended into an incoherent rumble. These were the sounds that fetched Chip around the corner of the jail-building, and he saw men spilling down the street, stirring the dust and crowding from boardwalk to boardwalk in one great formless wave that rolled relentlessly forward. Lariats were being brandished aloft and guns were banging as men fired at the sky, and Chip knew then that there was very little time left if he was to save Sam McAllister.

That made it a desperate moment for Chip, a timeless moment when he could formulate no plan, but there was one fact he noted and it gave him his cue. Most of the men of this mob had masked themselves with bandannas, though others too drunk to be mindful of future consequences, had made no effort to conceal their identity. Seeing that, Chip went sidling along the boardwalk, working toward the advancing mob but hugging the shadows, and as he moved along he hauled his own bandanna up over his nose, knotted it tightly and tugged his sombrero low. Thus he blended into the vanguard of the mob and became part of it, and thus he went back up the street, jostled and pushed along.

A dim light burned to the front of the jail-building, and a burly man bulked in the front doorway as the mob approached. This was Sheriff Frank Busby, and he held up a protesting hand, shouting, "Now, boys! Now, boys!" Swept back into his own office by a tide of men, he went down under the weight of them, and somebody brandished a ring of keys and cried, "I've got 'em!"

It was Chip's thought that Tumblerock's sheriff had made no real effort at defending his prisoners, and he pigeonholed that fact for future reference. Now he was only concerned with what was coming next, for the men were streaming back into the cell corridor, milling before the door of the only occupied cell while keys were tried until the right one was found. Then they were into the cell and striving to lay violent hands upon the two prisoners.

Chip was one of those who pressed inside. In this threshing darkness, men were shapeless, bulking smears of motion, but he made out Ute Kincade, who was struggling wildly and bellowing all the while, his voice frantic, his mouthings meaningless. But out of Kincade's cries, Chip caught the name of Seton Alessandro, and he wondered about that. Sam McAllister had put his back to a corner and was making a silent, hard-slugging defense, but as the oldster came lunging forward to put poundage behind a blow, Chip tripped him neatly and pounced upon him.

He got Singin' Sam's arms twisted behind the man, and he hauled Sam to a stand and held him pinioned in this fashion. Others were also struggling to get a hold on Sam, but Chip said fiercely, "I've got him, and I can handle him!" He propelled Sam toward the cell door and out into the corridor which was now crammed with men. Chip shouted, "Make room! I've got to get outside with this jigger!" Sam was still struggling wildly, and Chip whispered through the muffling bandanna, "It's me—Chip."

Sam didn't make the mistake of ceasing to struggle. He still writhed in Chip's grasp, but there was no real effort in his attempt to break free, and Chip knew that Sam had understood. Behind Chip, others were hauling Ute Kincade toward the outer door, and thus they burst once again into the night, forcing their way to the center of the street where a score of men milled around them.

This much Chip had succeeded in doing; he had joined the mob and gotten his hands on Singin' Sam, but it came to him now that nothing had really been gained; for the two of them were surrounded and those ropes were being held aloft again, and somebody shouted, "The big cottonwood down by the Eureka Saloon! That'll make a good hangtree!"

That cry must have given Ute Kincade the strength of desperation. One instant he was struggling in the grip of two or three men; the next instant he had broken free and was running, striking out wildly to left and right and clearing a lane for himself. And instantly every man of the mob was turning to run after him. They went howling at his heels, but Kincade had broken through the fringe of the mob and was clattering down the boardwalk, but, comparatively free, he was in greater danger than before. For now there was room for shooting, and a dozen guns spoke at once; and Kincade seemed to leap into the air and half turn around, and then he went sprawling in a grotesque heap, his eyes to the sky, his arms flung wide.

Thus had Ute Kincade died, and the sight sickened the very soul of Chip Halliday. He had had no love for Kincade, and certainly it hadn't been part of his plan to take the convict over Deer Lodge's wall with him. He knew that Kincade had had blood on his hands many times in the past, and he'd been hard put to restrain Kincade from spilling more blood in the days since the three had made their escape. But even Ute Kincade had deserved a death with dignity and a fighting chance to stave off that death. A mob's cruelty hadn't granted him these things.

But while such thoughts were crowding through Chip's mind, he and Singin' Sam were darting for the shadows that banked between two buildings on the far side of the street. For Chip had seen his chance and seized it. While every eye had been upon Ute Kincade, every gun aimed Kincade's way, Chip and Sam had been unnoticed for a moment, and that moment had put them out of sight.

Shortly they'd be discovered though, shortly the whole fury of the mob would be directed against them, and Chip's impulse was to run as fast as his legs would carry him. He put down that impulse with an effort, slowing to a walk instead and keeping a hold on Sam's arm to restrain him in like fashion. Boots hitting hard against the packed earth would have given the mob a clue to their whereabouts.

Beyond these buildings was an alleyway, and Chip eased into it. He hadn't taken a dozen steps before a figure loomed ahead of him. He tilted his gun then; he'd seen Ute Kincade die and he was determined not to die in like fashion, but Hope's voice reached him saying, "It's me!"

The breath went out of him in a gusty sigh of relief, and as the girl came closer he sensed her own breathlessness and the desperate urgency that gripped her. "I saw you join the mob," she said. "I've tried to keep an eye on you ever since. Come now; we must hurry."

"The horses!" Chip gasped. "Can you get the horses for us?"

"Too risky," she countered. "If there's a brain among those mobsters, the first thing they'll do is throw a ring around the town. But I know the place to hide."

Chip was content to let her lead the way. She knew this town; he didn't. Already voices were being raised in a shout on the street beyond, already boots were beating in a dozen different directions as the mob fanned wide to make its search. Hope, her fingers on Chip's wrist, paused before the rear of a big building whose odor identified it as a livery stable. "In here—quick!" she whispered.

Finding the back door unlocked, they eased inside, pausing in the deeper darkness to listen intently for any warning sound. Horses stomped nervously in stalls, the big front door was open, but the hostler had obviously gone out into the street to see the excitement. Hope guided them toward the ladder leading to the loft, and when they'd made the ascent they found the big second-story door at the street end of the building swung open. Crawling forward, they cowered beneath the protruding beam that was used for hauling baled hay to the loft—the beam with its dangling rope that made a grim reminder of the fate that awaited them if they were caught. Here they looked down upon the teeming street.

Men had started building a huge bonfire in the center of the street, hauling packing boxes and empty barrels from the nearby saloons to feed the flames. Whether some wild, meaningless impulse or a desire for light by which to make a more thorough search had prompted them to do this, Chip didn't know. But he watched the lurid light wash up the sides of the false fronts, saw the dark, restless silhouettes of men limned before the fire; and into the circle of light came a lithe, handsomely garbed man upon a beautiful black horse that instantly chained Chip's attention.

"Seton Alessandro!" Hope whispered.

Sitting his saddle with studied grace, Alessandro hoisted his hand for silence and commanded it so quickly as to impress Chip. The man cried, "Hear me, boys! I've just been told what's happened tonight. I can't condone mob action, but since you've managed to let one of the prisoners escape, I'm not happy over the prospect of a lawless man being loose in our midst, either. I'm offering one thousand dollars reward for the return of that man—dead or alive!"

Singin' Sam, silent until now, sucked in his breath. "A thousand bucks!" he exclaimed. "And there ain't an insurance company in these United States that would risk over five hundred iron men on my old carcass!"

Alessandro wheeled his mount out of the firelight with an almost theatrical show of horsemanship and was gone. Hope said, "We'd better dig into the hay pile. They'll be combing this town fine now. A thousand dollars!"

Chip knew she was right, and the three of them went burrowing into the hay, Chip lingering behind a moment to fork hay over the others before he himself made an effort at concealment. And thus they lay, listening to the myriad sounds of Tumblerock, hearing boots slog along the boardwalks below, hearing more shouts and curses and futile questions as men called one to another.

No more than twenty minutes later someone came into the stable. Chip could hear men moving around below, and he judged that there were two of them. Finally they came crawling up the ladder to the loft, one drunkenly waving a lantern. Keeping a tight hold on his gun, Chip lay as silent as possible, sure that the very sound of his breathing must carry to these two, sure that the hammering of his heart would betray him.

"Nobody up here," one of the searchers said thickly.

"Don't be so sure," the other retorted and picked up a pitchfork. He gave an experimental thrust into the piled hay, moved a pace and thrust again. The tines came close to Chip's legs, and he knew that if the man moved another pace that he, Chip, was going to feel the stab of that fork. Even if he could restrain a betraying sound, the searcher would be warned when the pitchfork struck something unyielding. Chip's finger tightening on the trigger of his gun, he made ready to fire, though he was clammy with the consciousness that the bullet that would save him might also betray him since the sound would likely fetch other searchers on the run.

The man with the lantern said, "Aw, let's get out of here, Buck. This damn' hay is gonna get me into a fit of sneezin' in a minute."

"All right," the other agreed, and tossed the pitchfork aside.

They went stumbling toward the ladder, and in another few moments they were gone from the stable. Outside, hoofs roared along the street, roared back again, but the sounds of shouting were dying. For possibly a full hour the three lay motionless, buried under the hay, and then Singin' Sam, who was near Chip, said, "I'm crawlin' out for a look-see."

The girl and Chip also shook the hay from themselves and came to a stand, and the three made their quiet way together to the loft door and had a look down into the street. Only a few men were in sight now; the others, Chip judged, had taken to saddles and hit the trails leading out of Tumblerock, convinced, likely, that their quarry had escaped the town.

No one had thought to move Ute Kincade's body. Not yet. It lay sprawled just within the rim of dying firelight, and Chip, peering hard, said, "What's Ute holding in his hand?"

There was no identifying the object from this distance. It was something Kincade had plucked from his pocket, perhaps because he had pinned some forlorn hope in the thing, perhaps because some queer reflex of dying muscles and a dying mind had made him do it.

Singin' Sam spat thoughtfully and said, "My guess is that he's holding an ace of spades. Now ain't that hell?"

7 : Perambulating Poison

They slipped out of the livery stable in a dark and silent hour before the dawn; most of the mob had dispersed by then, while those who were continuing the search had gone riding out of town. Huddled in the alleyway behind the stable, the three held a whispered conference, and Hope insisted on fetching horses. Chip's protests were countered by the simple argument that Hope was the only one of them who might walk Tumblerock's street unchallenged, but Chip became fiddle-footed and jumpy from the moment she left them.

Much had happened this night, and not all of it made sense to Chip. Waiting impatiently for Hope's return, he said, "A mob usually has to have a personal grudge to get itself worked up. You and Ute were strangers here, Sam. How do you figure it?"

Whereupon Singin' Sam told him everything—the dying tale of Gopher Joe Gravelly who'd known how to make money off an ace of spades—the scheme of Ute Kincade to capitalize on that tale—their capture and the fury that had built in Tumblerock's saloons during the long day. When he'd finished, Chip said, "Now it's beginning to add up. This fellow Alessandro wanted Kincade dead because Seton

Alessandro is obviously the man who pulled an ace out of his sleeve down in Grasshopper Gulch years ago. And Alessandro is willing to pay a thousand bucks for your scalp because he reasons that you know what Ute knew."

"As I see it, that makes me bad company for you, Chip," Sam said. "Likewise for the young lady. From here on out I'm a perambulatin' bottle of poison because Alessandro will be leery of anybody who rides with me, figgerin' I've passed the story on. So we'll take separate trails, once we get hosses."

"Nothing doing, old timer," Chip said flatly. "I'd only be hunting you down to get you out of trouble, anyway. We shouldn't have parted in the first place. But you savvy how it was. That scheme of shaking Strunk the other night wouldn't have worked so well if we'd all made the run. And somebody had to keep an eye on Kincade; I couldn't leave a kill-crazy wolf like him on the loose."

"But we'd better shake clear of the little lady for her own sake. Who is she, Chip?"

Now Chip told his own tale, and when he'd finished Singin' Sam said, "And you figger you saw her and some galoot totin' a dead man out of the house? Maybe she's already in bad trouble."

Chip shrugged. "I haven't asked her about that. Not yet. I can't help but keep remembering that on a range where every mother's son is gunning for our scalps, she's the one person we can call friend. That counts for a heap."

Hope herself put an end to their talk by appearing out of the darkness. "Sorry to be so long," she said, "but I played it safe and fetched the horses to the alley one by one. Ours were still at the hitchrail, Chip. And I found yours and Kincade's where you said they'd be, McAllister. I took the one with the saddle for you."

Mounting, they faded out of Tumblerock, avoiding the bridge lest men were guarding it, and they followed the creek northward until they came to a place where they could ford it. Once across the stream, Hope took the lead, aiming her horse in a general northeasterly direction, and Chip said, "Where you heading?"

"Back to the schoolhouse," she replied. "By hiding out near there for a while, we can get grub whenever we need it and lie low till the shouting dies. That mob will run around with its nose to the ground tonight and tomorrow, probably. But they'll get tired soon, especially when the whisky soaks out of them."

Once again Chip bowed to her wisdom; the miles fell behind and twice they had to hide out from groups of riders who were scouring the surrounding country. The dawn was in the east when they neared the schoolhouse, and when Hope mentioned that trail's end was not far away, Chip insisted on a slight change of plans.

"You go and get a roof over your head," he told Hope. "Me and Sam will unroll our soogans out here in the timber, close by. I think that'll be safer all around. There's a slight chance that Tate Strunk might have seen you, remember, just before I laid him out in the jail yard. If he comes back here, you'll have no real trouble with him as long as there's no sign of us around."

In this first light of the new day, she gave him a sharp look. "You wouldn't be intending to head for Forlorn Valley without me?" she challenged.

Smiling, Chip said, "Darling, I wouldn't think of going any place without you, now."

But that was a lie, and he knew it. Singin' Sam had called the cards right when he'd referred to himself as perambulating poison, and Hope Brennan, in the company of Sam and Chip Halliday, might also be marked for death. But this wasn't the time for argument; they all needed rest and the dawn was bringing another day. They chose a wooded spot for Sam and Chip's hideaway, but Chip made sure that the spot was within shouting distance of the schoolhouse. Hope left them then, and with their saddlers hobbled and the blankets spread upon the ground, the two men soon fell asleep.

The sun, climbing above the treetops, awoke them, and for a long time Chip lay staring at the blue vault of sky overhead, fashioning pictures out of the cloud wisps and thinking of all that had happened since he'd come to this Tumblerock country. Singin' Sam, nearby, stretched himself luxuriously and hummed a snatch of song, and Hope put in an appearance soon, bringing them a warm breakfast she'd cooked in the teacherage.

"I'll do a little riding this afternoon," she said. "I'd like to know how much activity there is in these parts."

Chip would have preferred to have her stay with them, and he found himself lonely after she'd gone, this in spite of Singin' Sam's garrulous company. Chip had never taken a girl seriously, but he'd known no girl like this one, courageous and competent, quick to think and quick to act. Already he owed her a mountainous debt, and he knew of no coin by which to pay her. She'd held him in contempt at their first meeting, deeming him a worthless wastrel who'd thrown away a fine heritage. He wondered if subsequent events had tempered her opinion.

Inactivity weighed heavily upon him that long afternoon. He rebandaged the wound Tate Strunk had given him that stormy night and found it healing nicely. He paced the width of this glade a score of times and made desultory talk with Singin' Sam. Near sundown Hope returned, and he ran eagerly to meet her as she slipped from her saddle.

"You're tired," he said. "Here, come sit on a saddle blanket."

Smiling, she accepted the invitation. "I think we can start for Forlorn soon," she reported. "Things are pretty quiet; about the only riders who are out are those who work for Alessandro's ranch. You know, I think that crew of his was the backbone of the mob last night. A bandanna over a man's face doesn't change the style of his clothes or the width of his shoulders, and I'm sure I recognized more than one as I watched you join the mob, Chip. They're a hardcase lot, those riders of Alessandro's, with a hardcase foreman, a fellow called Colorado Jack Ives."

Chip considered all this thoughtfully, then mustered his accumulated arguments. "I might have ridden away this afternoon and said nothing," he remarked. "I couldn't do that to you, Hope. But just the same, I'm thinking you'd better not come with us."

She glanced at him sharply. "We made a deal," she said.

"I know it," he countered soberly. "But things have changed. Hope, all the sign says that Seton Alessandro has taken personal cards. Alessandro wants Singin' Sam dead because he's afraid that Sam has gotten certain information that Alessandro needs hushed. I won't tell you what it is; anybody who possesses it is in danger from Alessandro. But don't you see that if Alessandro's riders spotted you with us, then Alessandro would always be afraid that Sam might have talked to you, told you what he knew?"

She whistled softly. "That does make a difference," she agreed.

"Then you'll stay here?"

"Ordinarily you two could get into Forlorn easily enough," she said. "You're fugitives and Clark Rayburn would grant you the sanctuary of the valley. Possibly he still will. But Seton Alessandro has power in Forlorn, too, since the Forlorners need him to get their cattle out of the valley and their supplies inside. I'm afraid that if Alessandro sends word that you're not to be admitted to the valley, the sentries will turn you back at the pass. That means that all three of us will have to sneak in, just as you and I originally planned, Chip."

"I promised to ask no questions," Chip said slowly. "But there's something I've got to know. If there's a real reason why you must get inside Forlorn, a reason that means you'll be safer inside than out, then we'll take you along. Otherwise I'm going to have to welsh on the deal we made."

She hesitated, but only for a moment. "I want to join Clark Rayburn inside the valley," she said. "He's my father."

That left Chip speechless at first. "Your father is the leader of the Forlorners!" he finally said. "But that doesn't make sense!"

"Brennan was my mother's maiden name, and the only name I knew for many years," she said. "But perhaps I should tell you the story from the first; then maybe you'll understand. It begins in a Catholic academy in Helena, and my earliest recollections are centered around that place. I wasn't of the faith, apparently, but I was treated kindly, though nobody can understand the loneliness of such a place except one who has been there. When I was old enough to ask questions, I was told that my mother was dead and that my father lived far, far away. They said he'd arranged to have me kept there."

"You never saw him?"

"Oh, yes. He used to come now and then when I was a small girl. I remember him faintly from those days—a tall, blond man with sad eyes. He'd take me out for the day; always we went to a noodle parlor in Helena's Chinatown, a very fascinating place with soft lights and silent, courteous waiters. I used to wait for those days, Chip, like the other children waited for Christmas. But when I was about twelve, he quit coming."

Singin' Sam blew his nose vigorously, and Chip, finding many questions but no words to voice them, held silent.

"The rest of the years don't count," Hope went on. "When I finished my schooling, I was qualified for a teacher's certificate. By then I was old enough to be determined to find out a few things. I went to the sisters who were heads of the school and demanded some facts. They showed me my birth certificate, and it was then that I learned that my name was Hope Brennan Rayburn. They said that my father had insisted that I be enrolled under the shorter name."

"And they told you where your father was?"

Hope shook her head. "They claimed they didn't know. Each month a check had come to pay for my tuition—a cashier's check from the Tumblerock bank. So that's what fetched me to Tumblerock six months ago."

Soberly Chip said, "Now I'm beginning to savvy why you'd dislike a worthless galoot like me. Shucks, I've thrown away the very things that would have been worth a million dollars to you."

Hope said, "The bank at Tumblerock was exasperatingly vague about those checks that had gone to Helena, so I went straight to the bank's owner—Seton Alessandro. He readily admitted full knowledge of the entire affair and told me that my father was the head man of Forlorn Valley. Alessandro had been acting as my father's business agent in regard to me, issuing those checks at my father's request. But Alessandro urged me to go away and forget about the whole matter. My father, he explained, had the same as accepted a prison sentence by choosing to live in Forlorn Valley."

"But naturally you didn't leave," Chip murmured.

"Of course not. The previous schoolmaster here had quit because of illness, and I finished out his term for him. And all that while I tried again and again to get into the valley. Finally I bribed one of Alessandro's bullwhackers to take a note to my father. In that note I urged him to come and see me, and he did. The night before last."

"Wait!" Chip cried and felt excitement tingle along his spine. "You mean your father came to the schoolhouse the night of the storm?"

She nodded. "He left just before I discovered you out in the yard."

"What did he have to say for himself, miss?" Singin' Sam asked.

"Like Alessandro, he urged me to go away. He claimed he

could never leave Forlorn Valley, and he said he'd quit coming to see me at the academy because he wanted me to forget all about him. I was young and free, he pointed out, and life held too much for me—far too much that I should be penned up inside the valley. I couldn't shake him on that point. I asked him why he'd enrolled me as Hope Brennan, and he said that too many people had heard of Clark Rayburn, the leader of Forlorn's outlaws, and he didn't want me saddled with such a name."

She sighed. "That's about all there is to it, except that I'm still going into the valley. Having seen him, I know that he's lonely and tortured and unhappy, and the possessor of some terrible secret that he doesn't dare tell me. I want to be with him, to make up for the years we might have had together. Once into the valley I can only hope that the same rule will apply to me as to all others—the rule that says that those who enter can never leave."

Chip, a man profoundly impressed, had listened intently to all this, and mingled emotions marked his reaction. But some pieces of a puzzle had fitted together, and he couldn't dull the memory of that storm-swept night and that brief, lightning-illuminated glimpse of the two slicker-clad figures with the dead man between them. He said, "Hope, are you sure—very sure—that there isn't something else you want to tell us—something that has to do with your need to get into Forlorn Valley?"

She met his gaze open-eyed. "No, Chip," she said. "Are you taking me with you?"

Chip sent a sidelong glance at Singin' Sam McAllister and saw something misty in the oldster's eyes. Singin' Sam nodded and in this manner cast his vote, and Chip nodded too.

"We'll chance it," he said. "The deal's on again, Hope. We're heading to Forlorn Valley."

8 : Fowl of a Feather

Today Tumblerock basked in a quiet somnolence as though the excitement of the night before had tired the town, sapping the strength from its main street and leaving it listless and jaded. The body of Ute Kincade had long since been removed and was now lying in the furniture store, which also sold coffins. The men whose angry roars had shaken the rafters of the saloons, those men who'd brandished ropes and marched against the jail, now clung to the shade, saying little and looking shamefaced. Tumblerock had been on a bender, and the inevitable reaction had set in.

But there was one man in Tumblerock who knew no remorse, nor any desire for inactivity. He was Seton Alessandro and he paced the width of his study like a caged jungle beast, a lean, restless figure in black velvet. From the depth of a chair, Jasper Fogg, more than a little drunk, regarded him wearily. "Sit down, Seton," Fogg said at last. "Man alive, if there's any news, your crew will be bringing it to you or sending you word with one of those sun talk gadgets you rigged out for them."

Alessandro said, "I'm growing stupid! I tell you I should have been prepared against the possibility that one of them might slip through our fingers. McAllister got out of town, of course. But if I'd had a ring of riders spread out in advance, we'd have had him bottled."

"He can't have gotten far," Fogg said. "And with your crew in the saddle, they'll pick him up."

"Somebody helped him; I'm sure of that," Alessandro said. "If we could find any sign, I'd set my hounds on the trail. I've wanted some hunting, and here's prize game. But the quarry's vanished from the face of the earth."

The buzzer, signaling that somebody was at the front door, whirred waspishly then, and Alessandro jumped at the sound, in this manner manifesting the high tension that held him. He said, "Go see who it is, Fogg."

The lawyer sighed, heaved himself out of the chair and went waddling into the hallway. When he returned a moment later, he said, "It's Tate Strunk. You remember I told you about him yesterday? He's the prison guard who was leading the hunt for those three."

"What does he want here?" Alessandro demanded.

Fogg shrugged. "A word with you, he says."

Alessandro did a moment's debating, his handsome, olive face puckered with thought. Then: "Show him in," he decided.

Fetched into the study, Tate Strunk stood with his sombrero crushed in his hand, his milkish eyes widening with awe as they took in this ornate room and the mounted trophies that decorated it. Reading these signs of opulence, he was like a stable boy granted entrance to the king's palace, a peasant in the presence of royalty. These things Alessandro noticed as he studied the burly prison guard, but there was more than he sensed, some depth of depravity to Strunk's character that made the uncouth man akin to himself. In their way they were fowl of a feather, Seton Alessandro and Tate Strunk, and Alessandro, recognizing this fact, was both reassured and made uncomfortable by the knowledge.

He said, affably enough, "Sit down, Mr. Strunk. We know

of you, of course. And we're very sorry for what the wilder element of this town chose to do last night. I presume you've already heard that one of your convicts was killed by a mob."

"I was here," Strunk said.

That fetched Alessandro's eyebrows up, and Strunk, sending a quick and calculating glance at Fogg, said, "I've come on personal business. Maybe we should do our talking alone."

"Mr. Fogg is my attorney," Alessandro said. "It is perfectly all right to speak in front of him. Do I infer that you were in town during the—ah—trouble?"

"I came back to Tumblerock yesterday afternoon," Strunk said. "I learned then that two of my three birds were in jail. But I didn't tip my hand to the sheriff. I waited up by the jail, and, just as I expected, Chip Halliday showed along to make a try at busting Sam McAllister out of the jail."

Fogg said, "There you are, Seton. Outside help."

Alessandro sent the lawyer a dark and silencing look. "Yes, Mr. Strunk?" he said.

"I got Halliday under my gun, but I made the mistake of turning my head for a minute. About that time a mountain landed on me and the lights went out. When I woke up, Kincade was out in the street, dead, riders were galloping around like crazy, and the fuss was all over."

Alessandro smiled bleakly. "You shouldn't have turned your head, Mr. Strunk."

"Someone came walking up behind me," Strunk said. "I had one look at her. It was a girl—a girl I'd seen before, out at a schoolhouse northeast of here. That was the night of the big rain. And if I ain't mistaken, she was hiding out one or more of those jailbirds then."

"Schoolhouse?" Fogg livened with interest. "Seton, that would be Hope Brennan!"

Alessandro seated himself at his desk, his fingers drumming thoughtfully on the polished surface. "Hmmm," he murmured reflectively. Then: "This is all very interesting,

Mr. Strunk. But Sheriff Busby is the man you should take your information to."

Strunk said, "Telling you this ain't all that brought me here. I've got a question or two to ask. First off, can you tell me anything about a rider who might have come this way about six months ago, heading for Forlorn Valley? Feller called Justin St. John?"

Alessandro shrugged, keeping his face as wooden as before. "The name means nothing to me. And many riders have headed for Forlorn Valley at one time or another. Some call it the valley of vanishing riders. This St. John was an outlaw?"

"Not by a long shot," Strunk said. "He was a special agent of the government of Montana, an ex-cowpuncher who does fancy chores for the governor that don't always go down on the records. You see, the governor has got an idea he'd like to throw Forlorn Valley open to settlement. There's a lot of good acreage going to waste up there, and it's fine cattle country from what they say."

"I see," Alessandro said. "And the governor sent this Justin St. John to clean the outlaws out of Forlorn?"

"No," Strunk said. "He sent St. John to find Clark Rayburn and to present a full pardon for all the Forlorners. And those Forlorners were to get first chance at the land, if they wanted to go on living in the valley. That would still leave plenty of room for newcomers. A smart old bird, the governor; he'd found the perfect solution for everything."

Alessandro held silent a moment. "Very interesting," he said. "And you think that Justin St. John is still in this vicinity?"

"He never showed back at Helena after the governor sent him to do that chore," Strunk said. "He's another rider who seems to have vanished when he hit Forlorn."

"You might ask Sheriff Busby about him," Alessandro suggested.

Tate Strunk seated himself, crossed his legs and began

shaping up a cigarette, taking a good long time at doing it and letting the silence run on until the feel of it was in this room. "I haven't been on this range long," Strunk said when he'd gotten the smoke going. "But I've ridden quite a few miles at that, and I've talked to a lot of people while I was looking for my jailbirds. A feller hears your name pretty often in this section, Mr. Alessandro."

"Meaning——?"

"They tell it that you're the go-between for Forlorn Valley, the middleman who sells Forlorn beef and sees that the valley gets its supplies. And you make a mighty fat profit going and coming. A nice deal, mister. But it would be all shot to hell if Clark Rayburn got that blanket pardon for the Forlorners and the valley quit being a land beyond the law."

The face of Alessandro stayed wooden; his eyes were expressionless as though a curtain had been dropped behind them, and he said tonelessly, "Are you insinuating, Mr. Strunk, that I saw to it that Justin St. John never reached Forlorn valley?"

Strunk smiled, but there was a shadow of fear in his milky eyes. "Justin St. John is dead, likely," he said. "Otherwise he would have reported back to Helena long ago. But I'm not such a fool as to come here accusing you of his murder, Alessandro. Don't you reckon I realize that I'd never leave this house alive if I had anything on you? But I think we're men who'll understand each other, mister. Do you follow me?"

"Not exactly," Alessandro admitted.

"The governor's concerned about St. John, of course," Strunk said. "He's so concerned that he's sent another man to search for St. John, and likewise, to deliver a blanket pardon to Clark Rayburn in place of the one St. John didn't deliver. I could tell you all about this new man, Alessandro."

"And you're mighty sure that I'm interested?"

"If you're not, we're both wasting our time," Strunk said

and came to a stand, picking his sombrero from the floor where he'd dropped it.

Alessandro let him get halfway to the door giving into the hall. Then: "Wait!" Alessandro cried, the first glimmer of respect in his eyes. "I'd like to hear what you've got to say."

Strunk said, "Am I working for you?"

Alessandro pulled open a desk drawer, dipped into it and produced a sheaf of currency. Laying the money on the desk-top, he said, "You appear to be a capable officer, and you're probably underpaid. You can call this an anonymous gift from a man who appreciates the worth of our public servants."

"That's putting it pretty," Strunk said and, scooping up the money, thumbed through it in a rapid count. Then: "The governor wanted to send another man in search of St. John, but that wouldn't have made sense. If one troubleshooter had come to a bad bend, another was likely to run up against the same thing. Only outlaws are allowed in Forlorn Valley; it followed that the governor had to send an outlaw up this way."

"Where could he get one he could trust?"

"That was the rub," Strunk admitted. "But it happens that the governor and a jigger named Iron Hat Halliday, a big stockman over in the east end of the state, were saddle pards forty years ago. Ah, you're beginning to see the light! The governor told his troubles to old Iron Hat, it seems, and Halliday's kid, Chip Halliday, volunteered for a scheme that had been cooked up. Oh, it was to be airtight. Chip Halliday was jailed for rustling his father's cattle, and Singin' Sam McAllister was caught in the same net. The two of 'em drew short terms at Deer Lodge. Last week they went over the wall; that was all fixed, but it looked like a genuine break. Do you see the scheme? The papers have been screaming the whole story; everybody figgers that young Halliday is a genuine jail-breaker and an all-around no-good hellion. And Halliday and Singin' Sam have headed straight for Forlorn

Valley—a pair of outlaws claiming sanctuary. It's fool-proof!"

"What about that third party, Ute Kincade?" Alessandro asked.

"He was the fly in the soup, I guess," Strunk said. "Must be he got onto Halliday's scheme for escape and insisted on being taken along. Rather than throw over the whole business, Halliday let him come."

"But you were laying for Halliday at the jail last night," Alessandro said quickly. "Weren't your orders to only make a *pretense* of trying to capture him and McAllister?"

"I had no orders," Strunk said. "The only ones who knew the whole truth were the warden, the governor, Iron Hat Halliday, and, of course, Chip Halliday and McAllister. But I happened to run across a letter in the warden's office—a letter from the governor outlining the whole deal right down to the last detail. To keep the truth from slipping out, not even us guards were to know that Halliday and Singin' Sam were any different than the other convicts."

Alessandro said, "Yet you took the trail? What was to be in it for you?"

"There's a standing reward for anybody who goes over the wall," Strunk said. "When the escape came off, I got up a posse and went chasing those three. Me, I figgered as long as I'd never been officially told different, I could claim the regular reward if I bagged 'em. My job don't pay too well, Alessandro, and a man's got to make his own opportunities. And then, yesterday, when I found out that McAllister and Kincade were in jail here, I figgered a new play for myself."

"Some blackmail?" Alessandro guessed.

Strunk shrugged. "Call it what you like. When I got Halliday under my gun, I had him where the hair was short. He didn't want McAllister strung up by no mob, that was a cinch. He would have promised anything in the world to get me to go around to the sheriff and arrange to have the prisoners removed pronto. And Halliday's the kind of fool

Norman A. Fox

who'd have later paid off on any promise he made. But before I could start making a deal with him, that damned girl showed up, Halliday jumped me, and the game was over."

"And now——?" Alessandro asked softly.

"Now I see a new game shaping up—a bigger and better game for Tate Strunk. You can use a man like me, Alessandro. You don't want Chip Halliday reaching Clark Rayburn in Forlorn Valley, and you've likely put your own men to stopping Halliday. But seeing as Justin St. John had disappeared, if Halliday does likewise, the governor will start pawing up some sod and maybe burst this range wide open with an investigation. But no questions can be asked if *I* nail Halliday; that's part of my job. The warden will kick himself for not letting me in on this little play, but that won't change anything. Do you see what I mean?"

"I see," said Alessandro. "But I'm not giving you any orders, Strunk. I don't believe I have to. But if you do your official duties well, drop back here and see me. I might have another anonymous donation."

"Sure," said Strunk, and picked up his sombrero again. "I'll be guarding the gate to Forlorn Valley, mister. If I know anything of the way of men on the dodge, Halliday and McAllister will lay low today and start moving again about nightfall. And we know where they'll be heading."

He left then, and after the great outer door had slammed behind him, Jasper Fogg, stirring in his chair, said, "Are you sure you can trust him?"

"He's after the biggest payoff," Alessandro said. "And I'm the man who can give it to him. Besides, he's still operating on his own; you're my witness that I gave him no orders. Yes, I think Tate Strunk will be of value to us, Fogg. So Halliday and McAllister are troubleshooters for the governor! An hour ago I wanted them dead because I figured they knew the truth about that ace of spades. Now I've got a better reason. And the Brennan girl is involved in this too, eh? I'm wondering, Fogg, wondering . . ."

• 78 •

Fogg said uneasily, "I don't like our mixing up into a deal that may bring the governor howling at our heels. That's a pretty big chunk to chew, Seton."

Alessandro said, "Do you think I'm throwing away what I've got here? Do you think I'm going to stand aside and let the Forlorners be pardoned? No, Fogg; it's too sweet a game to let slip through my fingers."

He headed toward the door. "I'm going to find Colorado Jack," he said. "He rode in a while ago, and I suspect he's still in town. I'm giving him a special job to do. He's going to play sentry at the pass to Forlorn Valley. If Strunk fails, Ives will be my sleeve ace. There can be no slipup this time. I want Chip Halliday and Singin' Sam McAllister dead."

9 : The Devil's Pawns

When Seton Alessandro had gone from the room, Jasper Fogg sat in silent contemplation, trying to forget the core of fear that centered his whirling thoughts, trying to marshal something tangible out of reasoning so that he might bolster himself. He'd had more than his share of the free whisky that had been dispensed last night, though he'd not been with the mob in its deadly march. By diverse ways he had succeeded in keeping quite drunk since, but now his mouth was beginning to feel fuzzy, and the fear kept revolving in his mind and prodding at the pit of his stomach.

He fell to studying this room, seeking to reassure himself as to the might of Alessandro by gazing upon these outward signs of his opulence. He began recalling the many years he had served the man; he had been in Tumblerock long before Seton Alessandro had first appeared, fresh from the Grasshopper Gulch diggings with enough money to make him needful of a lawyer's skill in handling it. There had been a professional man's pride in Jasper Fogg then, and he had given Alessandro a full measure of loyalty. But somewhere in those years had been that first deal that wouldn't meet the light of day. It hadn't amounted to much. But it had been a beginning. Now there was a long and shadowy past behind Jasper Fogg, a backward trail studded with many empty whisky bottles and a hundred deals that were best forgotten.

Aloud Fogg said, "His pawn, that's what I am. That's what we all are! Damn him! Damn him!"

The sound of his own voice startled him, and for a moment he was weak with panic. But the echo of Alessandro's boot heels had long since faded, and Fogg had heard the great outer door close behind the man. The lawyer's eyes flitted to the wine decanter on Alessandro's desk; he fought a silent battle with himself, and then he sloshed a glass full of the red liquid and downed it, wincing as he did. He was a whisky drinker by choice, and this made a poor substitute.

But at least the wine dispelled some of the chill in his stomach, and when the fumes rose he knew a measure of reassurance, and he waddled into the hall and let himself out of the house and went stumbling down the hill. Twice he sprawled headlong before he reached the bottom, and each time he picked himself up and carefully brushed his shapeless suit. When he reached the first of the buildings, a general store, there was a row of men keeping to the shade beneath its wooden awning, and one said, "Look at the old coot. So drunk he can't keep his feet on the ground."

Jasper Fogg came to a stop and regarded them all owlishly, framing a cutting retort but leaving it unspoken. Thrusting his shoulders back, he went angling across to his office, taking each step carefully and making a ludicrous show of sobriety. But the keyhole eluded him and it took a full minute before he let himself into the cubbyhole of a room. A rolltop pigeonholed desk of ancient make stood against one wall, a small iron safe flanked it, and there were filing cases and a swivel chair and a framed, flyspecked law certificate that hung slightly askew. Fogg drew the shade on the big bay window that fronted on the street and wished that he'd thought to do this before he'd left. It was oven-hot in here; and he slumped into the swivel chair and loosened his string tie and removed his shoes.

For a long while he merely sat, wishing mightily for a drink. Then he drew paper before him, reached for a pen and began writing. He had to hoist the shade then, to allow himself light; his eyes weren't as good as they used to be, and he made a mental note to see about a new pair of glasses the next time he went to one of the larger cities. From where he sat he now had a partial glimpse of the house of Alessandro, and he kept his eye on the trail leading from it as his pen scratched noisily.

He had written: "To the Governor of Montana." Beneath this he penned: "Sir: To salvage some small bit of decency from the wreckage of a conscience and a career that once were unblemished, I take my pen in hand. You are doubtless interested in the fate of a certain Justin St. John, commissioned by yourself to enter Forlorn Valley on secret business. You will likewise want any information available concerning Chip Halliday and Sam McAllister who are at present engaged in a like mission. Therefore I set these facts upon paper. . . ."

There was more, much more, sheet after sheet feeling the weight of Fogg's pen. Usually he wrote with one eye on that trail from Alessandro's house, though sometimes he became so carried away by the flow of composition that he forgot all else, and several times he started nervously, recalled to reality by the beat of boots against the walk beyond his door. But such passersby as were daring the afternoon sun paid no heed to him, and at last his letter was finished.

Placing the missive in a large envelope, he sealed it and scrawled the governor's name upon it. Then he spun the dial of his safe, swung back the door and thrust the letter inside. Remembering that one other man, Seton Alessandro, also knew the combination of this safe, he buried the letter deep beneath other papers, locked the safe again and returned to the swivel chair.

Seated here and facing the street, he saw Alessandro come striding down the hill then. At the bottom of the slope Alessandro angled off and was lost from sight, and Fogg guessed that the man had turned in at the jail-building. Presently Alessandro came into view again, poising on the edge of the boardwalk and talking to Sheriff Frank Busby. No word of this conversation carried to Fogg, but he could see Alessandro gesticulating in that Latin way of his, Busby nodding solemnly and putting in a word or two. Busby disappeared then, but very shortly he was upon the street astride his horse, and he went riding away, heading east.

Coming down the street, Alessandro paused in Fogg's doorway, leaning against the jamb and regarding the lawyer with half-lidded eyes. Alessandro said, "I sent Colorado Jack riding."

"And Busby, too," Fogg said. "I saw you talking to him."

Alessandro smiled. "That was still an extra precaution. Supposing both Strunk and Colorado fail and Halliday and McAllister get to Clark Rayburn in Forlorn? You know that Rayburn's been trying to kick over the traces. Now that Hope's here, he'd leave the valley if he could. But he won't now. He won't dare. When Frank Busby comes riding back to town, Clark Rayburn will be sealed in Forlorn for life. The governor's pardon wouldn't cover a killing that happened since the pardon was issued, would it?"

Wise in the ways of this man he served, Jasper Fogg thought he saw the shape of this latest scheming of Alessandro's and he said, "I don't like it, Seton! You need Rayburn in Forlorn; he keeps those valley ranchers in line for you, but he doesn't deserve any part of a frame-up like that. It isn't human for one man to hate another as much as you hate Rayburn."

Alessandro's eyes darkened, and there was something about him to remind Fogg of a storm gathering above the Tumblerock peaks. "My hate is my own affair, Fogg," he said. "Just remember that. And another thing. The wine decanter had been lowered when I came back into the study. You've got to quit this drinking, understand! You're no good to me or to yourself when your mind's clouded with booze."

Some ancient spark of manhood flaring deep within him, Fogg said, "Is that what's worrying you? Or are you perhaps just a little afraid of me? They say that rats desert a ship when it begins to sink. Are you remembering that, Seton?"

Alessandro bridged the little room in a single stride, and he cuffed Fogg across the mouth with the back of his hand, cuffed him hard. "Don't even *think* of double-crossing me," Alessandro said. "And don't ever put anything like that into words again!"

He went stalking out of the office, and Jasper Fogg sat looking after him. There was the taste of blood on the lawyer's lips and a great hate and a greater anger in him, but the spark that had flared so fitfully had died out. He was an old man, but never had he felt the weight of his years so much as in this bleak moment. . . .

Midafternoon found Colorado Jack Ives far beyond Tumblerock and following a lonesome trail to carry out Seton Alessandro's latest order. The unreeling miles had brought him into that lesser valley that lay to the south of Forlorn; he had skirted Alessandro's ranch buildings and noticed the deserted look of them. Alessandro's crew was out scouring the range for sign of that quarry whom Ives was supposed to corner. This Ives knew, for he'd been with those hardcase riders most of last night and this morning, returning to Tumblerock only to report and to receive a new and more definite assignment.

Always a grim man, Colorado Jack was grimmer today, his weathered face set in hard lines. He was to ride to the pass leading into Forlorn Valley and take the place of the sentry that Clark Rayburn would have posted there, substituting for the man by force if the name of Seton Alessandro wrought no magic. And there he was to wait until Chip Halliday and

Singin' Sam McAllister put in an appearance. That might be today, might be a week from now. Ives had his gun—and his orders.

Thus another pawn was being moved upon the giant chessboard of Alessandro's scheming, but this pawn differed from Jasper Fogg. Colorado Jack Ives possessed a will of his own and a distaste for the task at hand that was bringing him to the edge of open revolt. Also he was tired, and that made him testy. Coming into one of those parklike clumps of trees that dotted the floor of this Bear Creek Basin, he bowed lower over his saddle horn to avoid the sweeping branches that canopied the trail, and here he found a rider waiting, sitting a saddle in patient silence.

"Jack!"

Pure instinct swept his hand to his gun, and then he let his fingers fall away as he said in astonishment, "Lia!"

Out of that sinister house of Alessandro's, Lia Alessandro looked less like some fragile Oriental flower. She wore the same jodhpurs and silken white shirt she'd worn yesterday, and she'd donned a short jacket as well. But the sunlight, filtering down through the foliage, touched her face, and it was open and frank and altogether American. Or so it seemed to Colorado Jack. She was many women, he reflected, and was sober with the thought that he loved all of them.

He said, "What are you doing here? Don't you know that it might not be safe today; the range is crawling with riders."

"I've been waiting for you, Jack," she said simply. "You see, I heard him talking in his study today, and I knew he would be sending you this way."

Fear touching him, he said, "Does he know you were eavesdropping?"

She shook her dark head. "But I heard everything he planned. Jack, are you going to do this thing he wishes?"

He lowered his eyes. "I've tried to make you understand that I haven't much choice."

Jogging her horse nearer, she reached and laid her hand in his. "Jack, is there blood on this hand?" she asked.

"A man died last night," he said. "Riddled with bullets right down in the main street of Tumblerock. Liquor triggered those guns, Lia, and I'm the man who saw that the liquor was passed around."

She shuddered. "I know what happened," she said. "He was a wicked man, that Ute Kincade, and he had killed other men. But did *you* shoot at him, Jack?"

He shook his head. "I couldn't bring myself to do it. Whatever Ute Kincade did in his life, he never done anything to me."

"But now are you going to shoot this Chip Halliday and Singin' Sam McAllister?"

Again he lowered his eyes, saying nothing.

"Listen," she said and told him of Tate Strunk's visit to Seton Alessandro and of the things Strunk had told Alessandro about the scheme by which the governor had hoped to place Chip Halliday beyond the gateway to Forlorn Valley.

"You see!" she cried. "Shoot them and you are an outlaw yourself. Ah, he didn't tell you that, did he? But I am thinking of other things besides what the law will do to you if there is blood on your hands. I am thinking of *us*. Do we want the ghosts of dead men between us, darling?"

He said hoarsely, "The thing that first put me into Alessandro's power was no real sin, Lia. But there are chores I've done for him that have tangled me deeper and deeper into his web. But I've never notched my gun for him, believe me."

"And you never will," she said firmly. "We are riding far away, you and I. And we are starting now."

"But we can't; I've told you that!" he said. "He'd find us wherever we went, and he'd smash our happiness to pieces."

She said, "All that has changed, I think. What I heard when I listened to him and Strunk today opened my eyes to something I've been blind to. Now there is a name that I can whisper to him, and it will make him leave us alone."

But still his doubt was strong. "He wouldn't count the cost," he said. "He'd hunt us down."

She said, "I can't go back now, Jack. Not to the house or the ranch. You were right about him; he's cat cruel, a wicked and vicious man. I'm afraid of him. So if you will not come with me, I must run away alone."

That swerved him as no other argument could have. He threw back his shoulders and he said, "Where you ride, I ride with you, dear. Whatever chances you take, I take too."

Thus the decision was made, and they went jogging out of the trees and then rode stirrup to stirrup, the sun in their faces and the sun in their hearts. They had no definite trail to take, and they unconsciously headed north, for to the south was Seton Alessandro and the shadow they sought to escape. Once Ives said, "Do you know, I feel younger today than I have in years. Can you forget there's gray in my hair?"

She was like a child going out to explore the wide, beautiful world. She said, "I like your gray hair, darling. It makes you look distinguished."

But a thought had shadowed him, turning him somber again, and he said, "I'm afraid there's one last thing we must do before we leave this range. We've got to find Halliday and McAllister and warn them. You see, if they're lawmen in disguise, they'd count a man like Alessandro as their friend. They might even come to him for help if the chase got too hot. If I let them do that, I'd always feel as though I'd trapped them myself."

She said, "Now I know why I love you. It's because you think of things like that."

They kept forging northward, and when the dusk began to gather they were nearing the place where the walls of this valley started pinching together and the trail to tilt upward into the pass to Forlorn. Ives had kept an alert eye for riders and had been surprised to see none of Alessandro's crew all through the hours. Pulling off the trail into timber, the two came into the shadow of a low cutbank and dismounted. Ives said, "We could probably even risk a fire here. In any case, we'll stay here through the night, and I'll keep a watch for anyone coming up the trail. Maybe Halliday and McAllister will be along by moonrise."

She came walking to him, and he took her in his arms, holding her close and stroking her hair. He said, "You haven't known a devil of a lot of happiness, have you, Lia dear? You've lived in that house and its shadow has darkened you, but we'll have all the years to make up for that. You'll never be sorry that you rode away today, will you?"

For answer she nestled closer to him. There was no time, no distance for them now, no other humans in this vast Eden of pine and mountain and sky. Not until the voice of Seton Alessandro broke the silence and brought them whirling around. Alessandro said, "Very touching, Ives. I had no idea you hid such a sentimental soul beneath that hard exterior of yours."

He was standing on the rim of the cutbank above them, and backing him were four of the hardcase crew that rode for his ranch. These men had called Colorado Jack Ives their foreman, but it was Alessandro who signed their paychecks, and Ives saw nothing but antagonism in their steady eyes.

Alessandro held a gun in his hand. He said, "I saw you saddle up and ride away, Lia. And since I've not been entirely unaware of the rendezvous you and your lover have been holding in my house lately, I rather suspected whom you were going to meet. I've been watching you both through field glasses for hours. When Ives fetched you with him, I sensed that he wasn't on his way to carry out the order I gave him. So I came to hear what I could hear."

Over his shoulder he said to one of his men: "Rope them and take them back to the ranch house, Piute. And put them under lock and key."

In Colorado Jack Ives there was a desperate urge to try

for his gun, and it was only the nearness of Lia and the fact that she might be caught in a sweep of bullets that stayed his hand. The color had drained from Lia's face, but there was courage in her dark eyes. She said, "You will not lay a hand on us. If you do, I will tell what I know about Justin St. John —the man the governor sent here."

Alessandro laughed. "I'm afraid you'll have no chance to air whatever suspicion you are harboring." He glanced over his shoulder again. "Get them out of my sight," he ordered angrily. "I'll attend to them later. For the time being, I must wait here. Since Ives doesn't seem inclined to carry out his orders, I'll make a try at doing the job myself. If Halliday and McAllister are coming, they'll come up yonder trail."

He gestured with his gun, and there was nothing more he needed to say.

10 ⋮ Land Beyond the Law

Three riders neared Seton Alessandro's ranch at moonrise. They had taken a wary trail from the Bear Creek schoolhouse, this trio; they had kept to the brush and shadows and come unchallenged across the miles, and now they were nearing the last dangerous stretch to Forlorn Valley. Singin' Sam McAllister had ridden with his hand close to his gun, his ears tuned for any alien sound; and Hope Brennan, too, had taken on the nervous alertness of a seasoned fugitive.

Now, with Bear Creek Basin stretching before them and the moon edging over the eastern hills, Hope said, "We've been lucky so far. Not a sign of a rider. Let's hope that a night and a day in the saddle has sent them all to their bunks. With the moon climbing it's going to be mighty bright traveling."

"It's not as bad as it could be," Chip put in. "If riders will be able to see us at a distance, we'll be able to spot them, too. If worse comes to worst, we can always make a run for it."

Far off, from the direction of Alessandro's huddled ranch buildings, there came a faint and mournful sound, eerie and disembodied. Singin' Sam shuddered. "What's that?" he wondered.

"Alessandro's hounds," Hope explained. "He keeps a pack of the savage brutes for hunting. He's quite an accomplished hunter, I'm told; he's gone after big game in all parts of the world. Let's pray that he doesn't put those dogs on our trail."

They were moving forward as they talked, keeping their horses at a walk most of the time, now and then lifting them to a brisk trot, but saving any real bursts of speed for the hour when such a large edge might be desperately needed. The moon climbing higher, the basin's floor took on a silvery sheen, the intermittent clumps of trees looming blackly gargantuan.

It gave Chip the sensation of being abroad in a weird, dreamlike world. His eyes were everywhere, watching for any slight movement in the distance, and thus it was he who first saw the vague, bulking blotch up ahead.

Peering hard, he was certain that it was no group of riders who moved in the night. Low-voiced, he called the attention of the others to the object. Singin' Sam said, "Looks like a wagon," and Hope Brennan cried, "It is! It's another of those freight wagons! But the freighters went through yesterday!"

"Yonder's one that didn't," Chip observed. "Folks, maybe we're fools for luck. You figured out the one sure way of getting into Forlorn, Hope, and it looks like we've got ourselves a second chance to try that way."

"You mean we might slip inside the wagon?"

For answer Chip said, "Follow me—but not too fast," and he went trotting on up ahead. He had decided that boldness would serve him as well as a warier strategy, and he rapidly overtook the wagon, the lone bullwhacker who strode beside it casting a glance over his shoulder at the oncoming horseman, but showing no signs of anything but an ordinary curiosity.

"Howdy," Chip said as he came abreast of the man. "The sunlight too strong for you?"

This freighter might have been a twin to any of those who'd gone northward yesterday, for he was another bearded man with a broad-brimmed hat and a flannel shirt and pants tucked into high-legged boots. Flicking his long bull-whip, he said, "I'm some behind schedule. Was supposed to start out yesterday, but I stayed behind in Tumble-rock to shrink a tire on this wagon. 'Fore I was ready to leave, they was givin' away whisky in that man's town. Mister, were you in on that free bender?"

"I was in on it," Chip said grimly.

The freighter said, "I spent most of today sleeping in an alley. But with moonlight and a clear trail, I'll catch up on some of the miles I missed."

"I see," said Chip and his gun came into his hand. *"Get 'em up!"* he ordered.

The bullwhacker's astonishment manifested itself in a dropping of his bearded jaw and a stiffening of his burly body, and for a moment Chip thought the man was going to swing that long whip he held. Most of these freighters were artists with the whip, but this one chose to be discreet, letting the whip slip to the ground as he hoisted his hands.

"What is this?" he growled.

Chip raised his free hand in a beckoning gesture that brought Singin' Sam and Hope riding up. Chip said, "Here you are, folks. Free transportation to Forlorn Valley!"

"What about him?" Hope nodded toward the sullen bullwhacker.

Ahead was another of those parklike clusters of trees. "We'll take him there and leave him bound and gagged," Chip decided. "He'll give us no trouble, and he'll carry no warning to anyone else who might."

Singin' Sam said, "Here's a coil of rope, hangin' from the wagon. Let's get the chores done."

They herded the bullwhacker ahead of them to the

shadow of the trees, tied him, but not too securely, and gagged him with his own bandanna. Looking down upon the writhing figure, Chip said, "There's nothing personal about this, mister, and we mean you no real harm. You should be able to wiggle out of that rope in a few hours. But we need that much start."

Then he headed back to the high-sided freight wagon. Hope, who'd waited there, said, "What about the saddle horses? Shall we turn them loose?"

Chip came to a quick decision. "I think not. That was a good idea yesterday, but then we could have left the horses up in the hills. Turn them loose here and somebody might see them wandering around and get suspicious. Besides, I'd like to have them handy in case we want to leave this wagon in a hurry. We can stow the saddles under the tarp and lead the horses behind the wagon. Isn't it likely that somebody inside the valley might be buying saddlers and having the freighters fetch them in?"

"I suppose," Hope said dubiously.

The horses unsaddled and the gear stowed in the wagon, Hope and Singin' Sam hid themselves under the tarp, and, with the three horses tied to the tail gate, Chip tucked his trousers inside his boots, punched the shape out of his high-crowned sombrero, ran his hand over his stubbled chin and picked up the discarded bullwhip. He'd had no experience at bullwhacking, but he flicked the whip experimentally and the six-yoke of oxen began plodding forward.

Once again they were heading for Forlorn Valley, but though there was an added measure of safety in this new method of traveling, Chip found the slowness of it a drag upon his nerves. Also he had a cowboy's distaste for walking, and sometimes he hoisted himself upon the wagon and carried on low-voiced conversations with Hope and Singin' Sam. It was rough riding for them, he learned; this wagon carried bulky packing cases of various sorts of goods, and the bumpy trail didn't make such a bed comfortable. But that trail was taking them steadily northward and already the shouldering hills were crowding in closer, the lesser valley pinching together as the trail tilted upward into the pass.

The climbing moon told Chip that it was nearly midnight, and he was striding beside the wagon again when a figure loomed out of the night. At first Chip supposed it was the sentry whom the Forlorners kept posted here at the valley's gate, but there was moonlight enough to identify this black-garbed man who'd appeared, and though Chip had only seen him once before, and briefly, he recognized the man. It was Seton Alessandro, and he said, "Seen anybody on the trail tonight?"

Chip was keeping in the shadow cast by the wagon, but with the moon almost directly overhead, that shadow was far too narrow for his liking. These bullwhackers worked for Seton Alessandro, but doubtless they were independent freighters who took contracts from him; and the chances were that Alessandro didn't know all of them personally. Still Chip didn't risk speaking, but merely shook his head.

Alessandro said, "You'd better move along if you want to get beyond the pass before the moon sets. I heard that one of you fellows got bogged down in Tumblerock. Keep your nose dry the next time you've got a hauling job to do for me, mister!" He turned to stride away, then paused. "Say, what are you doing with these horses you've got hitched on behind?" he demanded.

Chip said, "Private deal with one of the Forlorners," and felt his skin crawl.

A frown of annoyance wedged between Alessandro's brows. "You must be new to this job," he said. "Don't you know that you fellows couldn't get inside Forlorn and out again if I didn't have a special arrangement with Clark Rayburn? You'll pay a cut to me on any deals you make."

"OK," Chip agreed, and snapped his whip.

The wagon moved onward, Chip sucked in a deep breath. Risking a backward glance, he saw Alessandro stalking off toward a clump of bushes and he thought, *So the kingpin himself was lying in wait for us!*

Ten minutes later Hope whispered, "Wasn't that Alessandro? I thought I recognized his voice."

"It was him all right," Chip said. "Keep quiet now. We'll likely be running into a sentry soon."

And where the trail was blacked out by the shadow of a high, overhanging boulder, a man reared himself not many minutes later, a rifle cradled across his arms. The man said, "Howdy. Your pards told me yesterday that you'd be along later. Pass through."

And in this easy manner Chip Halliday came into that land beyond the law, Forlorn Valley. The top of the pass wasn't far ahead; the oxen seemed to know the trail and they toiled along with a wall to the left of them and a drop-off to the right. Chip could look down upon a black oblivion of treetops, and sometimes he saw a flash of moonlight upon water where Bear Creek rumbled down out of Forlorn. Then the trail began tilting downward, and though it had many twists and turns it was a wide trail, a road of sorts, and the last of the moonlight found him at its bottom and upon the rolling floor of the vast, wide valley. Halting the wagon in the timber beyond the trail, he began unyoking the oxen, and when Singin' Sam and Hope crawled stiffly from under the tarp, he enlisted their help in hobbling the beasts.

"We'll go on by saddle horse," Chip announced. "It should be safe enough now, and it will certainly be easier traveling. The Forlorners probably need these supplies, but we'll tell them where they can find this wagon."

But they rode only a short distance that night. When the moon had set, they spread their saddle blankets and snatched some rest. The morning sun awoke them and they were soon in the saddle again, and now the whole glory of Forlorn Valley was spread before them, the pine-blackened walls on either hand reaching upward until they were lost in the remoteness of the sky, the grassy floor beneath them a rolling vista spreading ever northward.

It was breathtaking in its beauty, this valley. It was like a world apart, remote and removed from the petty strivings of that larger world that lay behind them, and Chip could understand now why the men who'd fled here had chosen to stay. He glanced at Hope and saw her solemn contemplation of all this, and he knew that she was beginning to comprehend what had kept Clark Rayburn here. For Chip himself this was a significant day; he had reached trail's end, that goal of careful planning. The completion of his mission was almost within reach.

Soon they were passing grazing cattle, sleek, prime beef, and sometimes they saw riders in the distance, but no man challenged them. They rode in silence, still awed by the spell of this majestic land; they wound through timber and skirted the babbling creek that flashed in the morning sunlight, and then, later, they saw a cluster of log buildings sprawled ahead of them.

"A town!" Singin' Sam exclaimed. "A regular town!"

"Forlorn," Hope said softly. "The town Clark Rayburn built."

Sam said, "It's a happy day for all of us—a day that makes me feel like singing." And the music came bursting from him:

> *O bury me not on the lone prair-eee*
> *Where the wild ky-otes will howl o'er me,*
> *In a narrow grave just six by three,*
> *O bury me not on the lone prair-eeee!*

Chip smiled, finding McAllister's mood contagious. "You can always gauge Sam's spirits by his songs," he said. "The sadder the song, the happier Sam is."

Singin' Sam said, "We're here, all of us. We've brought the little lady through safe, and in a few minutes she'll be in the arms of her daddy. Chip, why don't you tell her?"

Sam was referring to that secret mission the governor of

Montana had assigned to them, Chip knew, the mission that would make every man in Forlorn free, but he said, "A job isn't done till it's finished, Sam. I'd better do my talking to Clark Rayburn."

Then they were into the street of Forlorn town, jogging between two rows of log buildings. Ahead they saw the freight wagons that had come through that first day, lined up before what appeared to be a general store. Men were gathering in the street, eyeing the three of them curiously, and one came shouldering forward, a tall, golden-maned man, and even if Hope hadn't cried, "Dad!" Chip would have known somehow that this sad-eyed man was Clark Rayburn.

Coming down from her saddle, the girl ran forward, and Chip saw Rayburn stiffen for a moment and then open his arms to her. But even as Rayburn held his daughter close, the Forlorn leader said, "You shouldn't have come here, girl. We talked all that over the other night."

Hope was sobbing in her father's arms, and Rayburn lifted his eyes to the pair who'd brought her here. A craggy man, Rayburn had the look of one who'd lived long and suffered greatly. Chip said, "I'm Chip Halliday, Rayburn. And this is Singin' Sam McAllister. We both owe a lot to your daughter. That's why we fetched her here when she asked us to."

"We've heard of you," Rayburn said. "And we're not surprised that you headed for this valley. But I can't thank you for bringing my daughter. Most of the people here are wanted on the outside, and for their protection we have an ironclad rule. Those who enter must never leave again; that way the law gets no line on who is still inside. The only exception is made for the men who bring our supplies."

"We'll talk about that later," Chip said.

Rayburn was suddenly the host. "You must be tired and hungry, all of you," he said. "My cabin is just across the way. Come along, please. My people will attend to your horses."

Chip slid from his saddle, McAllister doing likewise, and the four of them crossed to a large cabin and stepped inside its open doorway. A grizzled man poked his head from another room and said, "I heard you, Clark. I'll have food on the fire in a minute."

Chip glanced around this homey room with its simple furnishings, then rasped his hand across his chin. "I could use a razor," he said.

Rayburn quietly furnished him one and showed him a place where he could shave. When that chore was finished, Chip found a table being set, and the aroma of fresh coffee and food was in the air. Here was hospitality, yet it was a queer, silent meal that followed, Hope keeping her eyes on her plate but stealing covert glances at her father. And Chip, sensing what was in the girl's soul, knowing her desperate wish to stay here and the fear that she might not be allowed to do so, smiled to himself, remembering the paper he carried hidden on his person.

And that was when Seton Alessandro came riding into Forlorn town.

They could see him through the open doorway, and as the man climbed from his saddle out yonder, Clark Rayburn stepped to the threshold and said, "Looking for me, Alessandro?"

"Some fugitives came into Forlorn last night," Alessandro replied without prelude. "They overpowered a bullwhacker and sneaked in with his wagon. Some of my boys found the bullwhacker bound and gagged down in the basin. The fellow spoke of two men and a girl."

"They're here," Rayburn admitted. "The girl is my daughter, Alessandro. But you've likely guessed that."

"And the men are Chip Halliday and Singin' Sam McAllister. I want them, Rayburn. My men are waiting at the pass; your confounded sentry wouldn't let anybody but me into the valley. I'll take those two out with me."

Rayburn shook his head. "They're outlaws and they've claimed sanctuary. I can't change the rules of the valley; you know that, Alessandro. They stay here."

Alessandro said softly, "Are you defying me, Clark?"

"I have no choice."

"Then think this over," Alessandro countered. "You're now a wanted man yourself, Rayburn. The law's got you marked as a killer, and even Forlorn isn't sanctuary for a man with blood on his hands. Sheriff Busby took a little ride for himself yesterday afternoon, and near the Bear Creek schoolhouse he found something interesting. The body of a murdered man. There wasn't anything in sight to identify him, but inside the white calfskin vest the man was wearing, Busby found some papers sewn. Those papers said the man was a certain Justin St. John, a special agent of the governor of Montana. And Busby's got good reason to believe that you're the man who killed this St. John, Rayburn."

A terrible wrath began to build in Rayburn; Chip could see it in the stiffening of the man's shoulders. Rayburn said, "You'll always find a way to hang a frame-up on a man, Alessandro. But this one won't work!"

Unperturbed, Alessandro said, "Busby will likely be writing a letter to the governor this afternoon, Rayburn. Once that letter is mailed, the state militia will be up here if there's no other way of dragging you out of the valley. Turn Halliday and McAllister over to me and that letter will never be mailed."

His anger making his voice unsteady, Rayburn said, "Climb on that horse, Alessandro, and see how fast you can get out of Forlorn Valley!"

"Very well," Alessandro said with a shrug. "You've made your choice, Clark."

Walking to his horse, Alessandro mounted, wheeled the animal and went galloping out of sight. Rayburn turned from the doorway then, and as he did so, Chip came to a stand, kicking his chair backward and unleathering his gun. For Chip was suddenly remembering that storm-swept night when he'd stumbled into a yard to see a man and a girl carrying a dead man between them—a dead man who'd worn a white calf-skin vest.

Chip said, "I'm beholden to you for not turning us over to Alessandro, Rayburn. So beholden that I'll likely always hate myself for what I've got to do. But you're under arrest, mister, and I'm afraid that goes for you too, Hope. You see, I happen to know that Alessandro isn't working a frame-up this time. You did kill Justin St. John, didn't you, Rayburn?"

Clark Rayburn said, "So you're a lawman, eh? Are you completely loco? How do you suppose you'll be able to take me out of my own stronghold? One shout and a score of men will be in here, Halliday."

"That," said Chip, "is the chance I've got to take."

11 : Stairway to the Sky

For a space there was a stricken silence in this little cabin, and it made a moment that Chip Halliday would always remember. Clark Rayburn stood poised on the balls of his feet, held in check only by the mute menace of Chip's gun. Hope had the look of one who'd been slapped into shocked lethargy, and even Singin' Sam seemed more than a little astonished by the swift shaping of events. For Chip there was no triumph, but only the empty sense of a duty fulfilled. In a gentler voice he said, "I'm not here to judge you, Rayburn. My job is to turn you over to the law for that."

Rayburn said, "The Tumblerock law of Sheriff Frank Busby and Jasper Fogg? The kind of law that Seton Alessandro will dictate?"

The name of Jasper Fogg meant nothing to Chip, but he could remember the sheriff's puny efforts the night a mob had come to take Singin' Sam and Ute Kincade from the Tumblerock jail, and he said, "It's pretty plain that Tumblerock dances to Seton Alessandro's tune. And if I ever saw hate in a man's eyes, I saw it in Alessandro's when he looked at you a few minutes ago, Rayburn. No, I'm not putting you into his hands. This is a matter for the governor of Montana."

Singin' Sam said, "Tell him the whole of it, Chip. Both him and the gal have got a right to see our hand."

Chip nodded. "We're doing a special job for the governor, Rayburn—the same job that fetched Justin St. John to the Tumblerocks. Our sentence to Deer Lodge and our escape over the wall were all engineered to give us a ticket to Forlorn Valley. We've fetched a blanket pardon for the outlaws of the valley. The governor wants Forlorn thrown open to settlement."

Rayburn was now as astonished as he'd been when Chip had first unleathered his gun. Rayburn said, "Does Seton Alessandro know this? Is that why he wanted to snatch you two out of Forlorn before you had a chance to show your hand?"

Chip shook his head. "Alessandro has a personal reason for wanting us dead. But he couldn't possibly know the truth about why we came here—not unless he's a mind reader."

"But don't you see what dad's driving at?" Hope spoke up. "Alessandro's the man who stands to lose the most if the Forlorners are pardoned! The people of this valley will no longer need him if that happens. Dad, I'm beginning to see a pattern to all this! Justin St. John fetched a pardon, but Alessandro found out about it and had him killed. Then these two came on the same business, and Alessandro discovered that, too. He must have! First he tried to talk you into surrendering them to him. Failing in that, he played another card. Sheriff Busby had found St. John's body, so Alessandro schemed to pin that murder on you. Maybe he thinks that with you turned into an outlaw, you'd tear up any pardon that was presented since it wouldn't protect *you*. Or maybe he figures the Forlorners will stand behind you and stay outlaw, all of them. Either way, the valley would still be beyond the law and would need Alessandro—need him more than ever!"

Chip said, "That makes sense, but it doesn't explain away one fact. When I rode up to the teacherage the night of the storm, I saw you and your father come toting the body of Justin St. John outside."

Hope looked at him long and intently, and at last she said, "You're *not* lying, are you? You really think you saw that?"

"Of course," he said.

"But you're wrong—very wrong. If I hadn't come to know you so well these last few days, I might think you were another tool of Alessandro's. As it is, I believe you must have been delirious the night of the storm."

"I was a little out of my head," Chip conceded. "I'll admit that. Yet it all fits! Your father came to the teacherage that night; you said so yourself—admitted he left just before you found me."

"Circumstantial evidence, Chip. It's hanged more than one person."

Clark Rayburn said, "No sense in arguing about all this. You can put up your gun, Halliday. Show me the pardon you claim you're carrying and I'll go with you to the governor."

Silently Chip passed his gun to Singin' Sam, and just as silently he seated himself and peeled off his right boot and began working at the heel of it with a knife he picked from the nearby table. Soon he prized a false center from the heel, and out of a small cavity he plucked a paper folded many times. "Here it is," he said, passing the paper to Rayburn. "This trick boot was left for me in a deserted ranch house near the pen. The governor thought of everything."

Rayburn opened the paper and scanned it. Then: "I'm your prisoner," he said. "Hope, you'd better come along, too."

"Dad," she said, "do you think this is wise?"

Rayburn shrugged. "Seton Alessandro is spinning his last web, girl. Part of his plan is that I should be an outlaw—but I've got to stay holed up in Forlorn if his scheme is to work. That much I'm sure about. In a sense, I'll be breaking my given word by leaving the valley. But I can't jeopardize the other Forlorners' chance at freedom by staying here. I'll risk the mercy of the governor. There is no other choice for me, Hope."

Chip said, "You'll probably be tried for St. John's murder, Rayburn. I want you to know that I've no choice, either. I'll have to testify as to what I saw."

Rayburn smiled faintly. "You'll have time for thinking before that day comes," he said.

Chip turned to the girl, his eyes making an appeal for her understanding. "You had your own reasons for not liking me at first," he said. "Now you probably hate me. I'm sorry, Hope. You were right when you guessed that I went into this thing because it promised a heap of excitement. But now I'm remembering that I likely owe you my life . . . and this is the way I'm paying you back."

She came to him, laying her hand on his arm. "Maybe I was wrong about your not having both feet planted on the ground," she said. "Can you understand that I might be a little glad that I was wrong?"

He shook his head. "I can only understand that I never bargained for a deal like this when the governor gave me this job."

Rayburn coughed slightly. "We'd better be riding," he said. And Singin' Sam McAllister, wise old man, cased the gun that Chip had given him, thereby putting his trust and Chip's into the hands of Clark Rayburn.

They came out of the cabin, and Rayburn had their horses fetched to them along with a cayuse for himself. When they were mounted, Rayburn raised his voice in a shout that brought men tumbling from the cabins, and women too, and a scattering of children. Waiting until a full score of people had gathered, Rayburn looked down upon them, and Chip, seeing the bearded faces and the bonneted faces turned to the Forlorn leader in respectful attention, knew that he was witnessing a loyalty that bordered upon the magnificent.

"Folks," Rayburn announced, "I am about to break a rule of the valley by leaving and taking these people with me. I may be gone only a few days—I may be much longer than that. I can't say. But if I don't return within a couple of weeks, you'll find a paper in my cabin—a paper bearing the signature of the governor of Montana. That paper will speak for itself. I'm hoping that I can be here to present that paper to you. I'd like that."

He paused, groping for words, and his voice choked. "However the cards fall, I'll be remembering you—all of you," he said. "So long, friends. *Vaya con Dios.*"

A murmur ran through the gathered Forlorners, but no man raised his voice in question or challenge, and Rayburn, wheeling his horse, pointed the mount southward, the three falling in behind him. Not once did Rayburn look back, but Chip saw the stiffened shoulders of this man who'd lived in Forlorn across the years and who now might be leaving the valley forever. And it came to Chip that it took a high sort of courage to do this thing that Rayburn was doing.

Soon the cluster of cabins had fallen behind them, and they were backtracking along the same trail that Chip and Singin' Sam and Hope had followed into Forlorn, skirting that flashing stream and winding through the scattered timber. They rode wordlessly, each silent with his own thoughts, but before the first mile was past, Chip, drawing abreast of Rayburn, said, "I'm wondering if it might not be wise to wait until night. Supposing Alessandro anticipates something like this? He might be waiting beyond the pass with his men."

"I've thought of that," Rayburn said. "We won't be going through the pass."

Chip asked no questions, but he was quick to note that Rayburn soon angled abruptly to the left, leaving the trail and following a crooked course that veered steadily eastward. They splashed across the creek, and the land began tilting upward, the timber growing thicker as they neared the valley's wall. Soon the high slant was towering above them, and Chip discovered that it was not as perpendicular as it had appeared from a distance. Now Rayburn began making a search, riding first south and then north again until at last he found what he sought.

"You've all been patient," he said with a smile. "Now you'll have your reward. For you'll see something that very few people have ever seen—a secret exit from this valley. I discovered it by accident many years ago; for the sake of security I showed it to only a select few on occasions of emergency. A series of switchbacks begin here—a sort of giant stairway to the sky. They are not noticeable from the valley floor, but they will take us to the top of the wall."

"The hosses too?" Singin' Sam asked dubiously.

Rayburn nodded. "It's touchy going in some places, but just follow me."

And so they began to climb, winding upward in single file, Clark Rayburn leading the way, with Singin' Sam just behind him and Hope coming next while Chip brought up the rear. Sometimes they followed a natural ramp, wide and with no noticeable grade, but sometimes they hairpinned into a narrow trail, a mere shelf clinging to the side of the wall, and in such places they had to lead their horses and move along slowly, the wall at one elbow, eternity at the other. Rayburn's cayuse had a strain of mountain goat, but the other saddlers, growing more skittish, had to be blindfolded.

Halfway up, they paused for rest, and from here they could look down into the valley, seeing the creek flashing in the sun, seeing the distant rooftops of Forlorn town with the smoke of many chimneys hanging lazily above the cabins. Then they were climbing to the sky again, and there came a time when the horses humped up one more rise and they stood at last on the top of the wall. Singin' Sam, sleeving sweat from his bald head, said, "There was moments when I sure craved a pair o' wings. Next time I think I'll take a chance on whatever may be waitin' at the pass!"

They rested again, and then they were into saddles and

heading southward. The way led from the valley's rim and down into a land thick with lodgepole pine and slippery with needles, a shadowy, palisaded land where only the westering sun gave them a sense of direction. Somewhere in the distance a waterfall made muted music, and once Chip thought he saw a bear lumbering off into the underbrush. Rayburn threaded this country with a surety born of long knowledge of the Tumblerocks, and when they worked their way out of the timber, they found themselves looking down into Bear Creek Basin.

"If Alessandro's at the pass, we've outflanked him," Rayburn observed. "What's your plan from here on out, Halliday?"

"We'd better likewise outflank Alessandro's ranch and Tumblerock town," Chip said. "If we can reach the railroad somewhere south of town, we'll flag a train to Helena."

"Night's comin' soon," Singin' Sam observed.

"And it isn't so very far to the schoolhouse," Hope said. "We can get a bite to eat there."

Within a few more miles Chip began to recognize familiar country, and he realized they were covering the trail he and Hope had followed when they'd come to the rim of Bear Creek Basin to watch for Alessandro's freighters. Again they rode silently, a queer cavalcade, prisoners and captors in a sense; yet the only bond that held Rayburn and his daughter was a given word.

Chip had charged them with murder, and they were going to the governor to answer that charge. He, himself, would be the key witness against them, yet Hope insinuated that delirium had given him that picture of the Rayburns carrying Justin St. John's body from the Bear Creek teacherage. And because their faith was so unshakable, he fell to wondering if they were right and he was wrong, and if that scene he'd thought he'd witnessed had indeed been some fantasy of that storm-swept night.

But no; he'd remembered seeing that white calfskin vest

on St. John, and Alessandro, in Forlorn Valley, had mentioned that same vest and the papers Sheriff Busby had found sewn inside it. A man didn't dream up details that jibed like that.

Chip shook his head. Here was a riddle with no solution, and he was still thinking about it when Hope said, "We're near the teacherage now. It might be better if I went on alone. I can get things quickly and make less noise than all of us would."

"You're thinking the sheriff might be around," Chip guessed. "He's supposed to have found the body near here."

"Busby's law has no claim on me," Hope pointed out. "It's dad that Alessandro's trying to frame. And don't forget, Chip, that you and Sam are still escaped convicts in Busby's eyes."

Chip made no further argument, but he watched her go with certain misgivings. He did not share her belief that Tumblerock law would leave her unmolested, and a feeling was beginning to grow on him that they were not alone in this tumbled land of rock and tree and sky. The gathering darkness swallowed Hope, and the three sat waiting.

"Danged if I don't think one of us should have gone along," Sam opined as he looped a leg around his saddle horn. He sat fidgeting for a few minutes. "Seems like she's taking a mighty long time."

A twig cracked nearby. "Here she comes," Rayburn said.

But suddenly Chip sensed that it was not Hope making her return, and his hand swept down to his holster before he remembered that he'd given his gun to Sam. Then it was too late. Four men had bulked out of the bushes, and one of them was Sheriff Frank Busby, a gun held rigid in his hand. "Get 'em up!" the lawman ordered, and there was no choice but to obey.

Thus they were taken prisoner, and Chip cursed the luck that had made them such easy prey. Expecting Hope, they'd attributed that one betraying sound to the girl's return.

They'd had their warning and misinterpreted it, and the only consolation lay in the fact that Hope hadn't been bagged with them.

Busby said, "So you're here, Rayburn. This is pure luck for me; I thought Alessandro had you bottled up in the valley. And Singin' Sam McAllister! And you, mister; I'm guessing you're Chip Halliday. One of you boys search 'em for weapons while the others fetch up the horses."

The search was made, but none too quickly to suit Chip, whose only wish now was to be away from here before Hope returned. Would she hear the voices and be warned? And did Busby guess that a fourth person had been with this party? Chip didn't know, but his disgust at being captured was tempered with a certain elation a moment later when the sheriff and his men, climbing into their own saddles, began herding the three prisoners ahead of them.

"Just aim those cayuses for Tumblerock," the sheriff ordered. "And remember that we'll be flanking you with guns lined on your briskets." He glanced at one of his deputies. "Sig, you cut straight across country to Alessandro's ranch with word of this."

Rayburn said, "So you're still doing Alessandro's fetching and carrying, eh, Busby?"

"There's a dead man in Tumblerock," Busby said. "The sign points that you're the one who killed him, Rayburn. You'll have your chance to make your say at the coroner's inquest. As for these other two, they'll roost in jail till Deer Lodge sends for 'em."

But Chip was already wondering if that was the way it was to be. Hope's theory was that Seton Alessandro had somehow learned of the mission that had brought Chip and Singin' Sam to the Tumblerocks. And Alessandro had reason for stopping any man who packed the governor's pardon. More than that, Alessandro had already tried to have Singin' Sam killed, and there was still that knowledge of a crooked ace of spades that had to die with Singin' Sam and any other man whom Alessandro might suspect of possessing it. All the sign said that Tumblerock town was a waiting death trap.

And so Chip Halliday came once again toward Tumblerock, came with the growing knowledge that he must never let himself be put in Frank Busby's jail. He rode with a wary eye, but there was no chance at escaping; Busby and the remaining deputies, crowding in close and keeping their guns ready, precluded that. There was nothing to do but ride along, taking this trail to its inevitable end.

The night came, and the first starlight and a rising moon damned any hopes Chip had cherished that full darkness might give him the opportunity he desired. The miles had unreeled steadily, the bridge spanning Bear Creek was ahead of them, and Tumblerock sprawled beyond. And because a sense of desperation had been growing upon Chip, he made his chance where there was no chance—made it in the middle of that wooden bridge.

Just for the moment the six horsemen were strung out more loosely than they'd been; just for a moment the lawmen were less wary, satisfied, perhaps, that within shouting distance of the town they had practically accomplished their mission. And in the midst of that unguarded moment, Chip rose in his stirrups and took a headlong dive. Clearing the railing of the bridge, he saw the dark waters rush upward to meet him. Above, the guns of Busby and his men began a frantic banging.

12 : The Tottering Walls

Seton Alessandro, riding down out of Forlorn Valley after being defied by Clark Rayburn, was as angry as he ever permitted himself to be, and coupled with his anger was a growing anxiety. A man given to scheming, he'd seen his schemes go wrong too many times of late and a faint webwork of worry was beginning to trace itself beneath his velvety eyes. That old feeling that the walls he'd reared were beginning to totter had taken hold of him again, and he forced himself to a cold appraisal of the facts and a desperate determination to face them.

Ah, but it had been a good thing he'd fashioned here in the Tumblerocks. With the gold of Grasshopper Gulch to back him, he'd grown richer when he'd found the need of Forlorn Valley for an outside man and filled that need. With Clark Rayburn installed in the valley, things had gone smoothly for many years; the Forlorners accepted Rayburn as a leader, and if some quibbled about the exorbitant cost of Alessandro's cooperation, there was always Rayburn to remind them that they had no choice but to string along. For Clark Rayburn was the man who'd sold himself to Seton

Alessandro on the turn of a crooked card, and Rayburn belonged to Alessandro, body and soul.

All these years Rayburn had kept a gambler's bargain, but of late Rayburn had been dissatisfied, anxious to leave the valley where he'd buried himself alive to serve Seton Alessandro. That dissatisfaction had stemmed from Hope Brennan's arrival in the Tumblerock country, Alessandro knew. He'd told Rayburn of the girl's presence, and that had been the first mistake. Yet so far Rayburn had rigorously held to his bargain.

Then Justin St. John, that troubleshooter of the governor's, had come riding. Alessandro knew far more about the fate of St. John than he'd intimated to Tate Strunk, and, in any case, St. John was dead and would never deliver a blanket pardon to the Forlorners—a pardon that would mean no more profit for Seton Alessandro. St. John was a gone gosling, and Alessandro had hoped to turn the man's death to his own advantage by pinning a murder upon Clark Rayburn. Yet had that been so wise? It would work if it scared Rayburn into staying inside Forlorn. But sometimes Clark Rayburn was unpredictable, and there was no knowing how he might react to what he sensed was a frame-up to keep him within Alessandro's grasp.

And now there was Chip Halliday and Singin' Sam McAllister to think about—that precious pair who'd penetrated into Forlorn Valley to finish the job where Justin St. John had failed. More than that, McAllister probably knew the story behind that crooked ace of spades, and if McAllister inadvertently told Clark Rayburn about it, Alessandro's claim on the Forlorn leader would be forever gone. True, he might still see Rayburn dangling from a gallows for the death of St. John, and there'd be a certain satisfaction in that. But the other Forlorners would be free, the valley thrown open to an influx of newcomers.

Unless . . . And now Alessandro smiled for the first time today. Unless circumstances shaped themselves so that the

Forlorners chose to protect Clark Rayburn, thus plunging themselves deeper into outlawry and exhausting the patience of the governor.

Here was a thought with which to toy, and Alessandro dwelt upon it, shaping and reshaping it with an artisan's skill, and in this manner he came riding to where a half-dozen of his crew waited in the north end of the Bear Creek Basin. A bearded, hardcase lot, they were hunkered around a spread saddle blanket, playing poker, but they came to a stand as he rode up. Singling out one, a hook-nosed man with a prominent display of yellow teeth, Alessandro said, "I've been meaning to tell you, Piute; you're foreman now in Colorado Jack's place. Did you get him and the girl back to the ranch without any trouble?"

Piute spat to one side, and nodded. "I left a couple of the boys to keep an eye on 'em. What's next?"

"I'm riding to the ranch," Alessandro announced. "You fellows hang around here for a while. If anybody tries to leave the valley, send word to me by sun talk."

"Sure," said Piute, and Alessandro rode on.

Coming down across the miles at an easy pace, he approached his ranch from the rear, and it was late afternoon before he made out the high outline of the big barn among the trees that almost concealed the place. Turning his horse over to one of his crew who loitered near the corrals, Alessandro headed toward the ranch house, but a whim made him pause before a high, fenced enclosure that abutted the back of the house. Within this enclosure he kept his hunting hounds, and he climbed to a runway that jutted from one side of the fence and peered over the pickets at the half-dozen black, big-bodied creatures that padded restlessly below. There'd been a time when hunting had filled Alessandro's days, and from this ranch he'd traveled to far and savage shores to pursue his hobby. Between such trips he'd combed the Tumblerocks with this brutish pack. Watching the hounds now, he promised himself that he'd find more time for them when he'd taken care of the troubles which now beset him.

The ranch house was a huge, sprawling, two-storied affair, not unlike his town house in many ways, and when he came around to the front of it, Jasper Fogg was just dismounting from a saddle horse at the gate. The lawyer said, "Ah there, Seton; I thought I might find you here. So Sheriff Busby discovered himself a body yesterday. But Busby isn't doing much talking. Still, I keep remembering you sending Busby off on a little pasear, Seton. Wouldn't be that the body is that man of the governor's that Strunk talked about?"

Fogg's round, pink face was more than a little flushed, and it wasn't only the exertion of the ride that had given him this high floridness. Angrily Alessandro said, "Come inside to do your talking, you drunken fool! Do you want to shout to the mountaintops?"

Another of Alessandro's crew lounged before the doorway to the ranch house, and Alessandro, nodding to him, let himself into a hallway that gave off into a study that was a smaller replica of the one in the town house. Here too was a fireplace and mounted animal skins, a gun collection and a teakwood desk that was twin to the one in Tumblerock. There was even a wine decanter, and Alessandro helped himself to a drink without offering one to Fogg. Seating himself, Alessandro said, "Halliday and McAllister got into the valley. I asked Rayburn to turn them over to me, but he refused, claiming the law of the valley came first. Does that give you an idea how things stand?"

Fogg must have drawn upon a long knowledge of Alessandro's ways, for he said, "I'm guessing that you've already found the means to fix that. Would Rayburn be the man the law will be looking for when word of St. John's death reaches Helena?"

Alessandro frowned. "I told Rayburn that Busby would be writing to Helena, but that's only a bluff for the time being. Still, if I can't keep Rayburn in line, then I must destroy him.

But who can I put in Forlorn in his place? It takes a strong man to keep that valley crew from biting the hand that's feeding them."

"Colorado Jack?" Fogg suggested.

Alessandro's frown deepened. "I hadn't thought of him. He and Lia tried to run away together yesterday. I've got them locked up here now. They're in love; that's the thing I hadn't counted on. But I'll tear that idea out of them, bud and root."

Fogg said, "I've watched these two, and you can't do it, Seton. You've played at being God so long that you've come to believe in your own omniscience. But there had to be a day when you'd bump into something too big for you."

"Think so?" Alessandro countered. "Then wait and listen."

He raised his voice to a pitch that fetched the man who'd been posted at the outer door. When this fellow stepped into the study, Alessandro said, "Where are you keeping Ives and my girl?"

"Separate rooms upstairs," the man said. "One of the boys is hunkering in the upper hallway to make sure they don't get away. And they won't be climbing through the windows. We picked rooms above the pen where you keep the hounds. Ives never was a hand with those dogs."

"Good thinking," Alessandro applauded. "I want the two of them fetched here."

A few minutes later the man and the girl were shoved into the study, Lia disheveled and wide-eyed, Ives defiant and showing the shadow of a beard stubble. Alessandro, coming to a courtly stand, waved them to chairs, but as he seated himself he reached into the teakwood desk, produced a fancy, silver-inlaid forty-five and placed it before him. His wave dismissed the two men who'd fetched these prisoners, and he said, "Perhaps I should begin with an apology. You've been badly treated, the pair of you. But you must understand, Ives, that it does something to a man when he finds himself losing a person who has been like a daughter to him."

His words brought a flare of hope to Lia's dark eyes. But Colorado's jaw jutted truculently. "You don't mean a word of it," Ives said. "This is just another of your damn cat-and-mouse games. Now start saying what you really want to say."

"And what would you like?" Alessandro countered savagely. "My blessing and a dowry?"

"We'd like to be rid of the sight of you!" Ives said. "We'd like to live our own lives in our own way—just as far from here as we could get!"

Alessandro spread his hands in a gesture of pained righteousness. "But first you should learn about each other," he said. "After all, you're really strangers. Lia, did you know that Colorado first came to me as a confessed criminal, one of the many who have headed this way in order to enter Forlorn Valley? Ah, but that's the truth, and Colorado doesn't dare deny it. I offered him a chance at honest work, a way to redeem himself. I made him my foreman. And he has repaid by trying to steal you from me. Is this the man of your choice—this outlaw who hasn't even gratefulness in him?"

"I love him," Lia said in a small voice, and this eternal answer of all womankind wrung a smile from Jasper Fogg, who made an unobtrusive figure over against one wall.

The dusk was crowding up against the windows now; Alessandro lighted the lamp on his desk, and his face became a hard mask of planes and shadows. "And you, Ives?" he said. "It doesn't matter to you what *she* is?"

"Of course not!" Ives snapped.

"Yet you should know, and you will," Alessandro went on, unperturbed. "Many years ago I made a trip to India. I did some big game hunting; this tiger skin in the center of the floor is a memento of that trip. They have an interesting manner of hunting in India: native beaters thresh through the jungle, flushing the game toward the hunter who has merely to sit in safety, waiting for his prize to appear. But you are not interested in an account of that, of course. It's Lia you want to hear about, and it was in Bombay that I found her."

He saw Ives's interest had quickened, and he drew a feline satisfaction from the man's intensity. "I was invited to put up at the Royal Bombay Yacht Club," Alessandro went on. "Bombay is the queen of Indian cities, and the Yacht Club is something to remember. But it was the slums that always interested me. My last night there, I hired a native *gharry,* a small buggy drawn by a single horse, and I visited those slums. You should see them, Ives. Filth . . . darkness . . . thousands of people crammed between bare walls on stamped earthen floors . . . men and women and children with all the loathsome diseases that ever afflicted mankind. Human life is cheap in India. And in this squalor, this sink-hole of all creation, I found Lia, a little tot, naked and dirty and homeless."

"You're lying!" Ives said, leaning forward in his chair.

"You think so? Yet that's where I found her, and I brought her home with me. Why? Some travelers adopt a young cheetah and fetch it away to raise for their amusement. I saw the possibilities of a nobler experiment. I would take this offspring of darkness and filth and raise her in a manner of an aristocrat and see whether a different environment would stamp out her low-caste heritage. I gave her a name—Lia; it sounded exotic and seemed to fit her, and I bestowed my own last name upon her. But the child has run true to type."

Alessandro spread his hands again. "Her parents? Who can tell? There are many religions in India, most of them based upon bloodshed and voluptuousness. For instance, the women of the followers of *Krishna* are taught that the highest bliss in heaven and on earth is theirs if they submit to the caresses of the holy men of their faith. Doubtless Lia's own mother, called upon to identify the child's father would find it difficult to—*Steady, Ives! Come out of that chair and you're a dead man!"*

The gun was in Alessandro's hand, and Ives, his face twisted with anger, sank back into his chair. Lia had pressed her face into her palms; her head was bowed, and dry sobs shook her. But still Alessandro talked on, using words as he might have used a lash, cutting and slashing and stinging until he was spent with the effort.

Now he said in a calmer voice, "I've told you this so each of you will know what he or she is bargaining for. Ives, are you still such a fool that you'll throw away your place with me for *that?"*

Ives was chalky white, and his voice trembled. "Someday somebody is going to kill you, Alessandro," he said. "If there's any justice under heaven, that man is going to be me!"

Lia's face was white too, white with humiliation and shame, but her eyes were alive with hate. "Jack said you were cruel, cat cruel," she said. "I didn't believe him. I didn't want to believe him. Now I know he was right. I was in the hall yesterday when you spoke to the prison guard, Tate Strunk. You are going to let us go, or I will find a way to tell who really killed that man, Justin St. John!"

Alessandro's shout fetched the two men from the hall. "Take them away," Alessandro said wearily, "and lock them up again."

After the prisoners had been removed, he sat hunched over his desk, a man turned older, a man defeated. He seemed to have forgotten Fogg's silent presence, and he mechanically reached into his desk and produced a small, faded tintype which he propped up against the lamp. It pictured a woman's face, dark and exotic. Beside this tintype he laid the gun, and for a long time he sat studying these two objects in mute contemplation.

Finally Fogg said, "So now you've got a choice to make. She knows something that could put your neck into a noose, and you're remembering that you've got to kill her to ensure her silence. But that picture stands between you and what you'll have to do. It's a hell of a choice, isn't it, Seton?"

Alessandro started nervously; across the lamp he looked at Fogg as though he were just discovering the man's presence, and he said, "You're gloating, damn you! You're laughing because you've seen me licked by her, and that pleases that shriveled, whisky-besotted soul of yours. I've told you too much about myself, Fogg. Far, far too much."

"Listen!" Fogg cried. "A rider's coming up. And in an almighty hurry, I'd say."

Out yonder hoofs were pounding, slithering to a stop, and leather squealed as a rider dismounted in the yard. Another moment and his boots were beating along the hall, and the man himself came bursting into the study. One of Frank Busby's deputies, he said. "The sheriff sent me, Alessandro. You'd better come to town. He'll have Clark Rayburn locked up in jail pronto—he captured him earlier tonight."

"Rayburn!" Alessandro said and came to a stand. "Rayburn's out of the valley?" And because this was not as he'd planned, he wondered how he'd fit this new development into his scheme of things. But with a flash of inspiration he was already seeing his way.

13 ⋮ By Whose Hand?

Chip Halliday, diving downward into the white-crested, raging waters of Bear Creek, had a breathless moment when he thought he was going to batter himself against the rocks studding this stream. He'd had no time to weigh the consequences when he'd gone over the railing of the bridge, no thought but to elude the lawmen who were bringing him to Tumblerock's jail. He'd acted on impulse, and now the creek rose up to claim him; he plunged under the water, feeling his shoulder scrape against a bulking rock, and then the current had a hard hold on him and he was swept along between the willow-fringed banks.

High up on the bridge behind, the guns were blossoming redly against the night; but the roar of them was blanketed beneath the greater clamor of the creek. Mountain snows fed this rampaging little river, and the cold shock of the water numbed Chip, sapping his strength away and turning his legs and arms to wood. He made no effort at swimming, only striving to keep his head above the surface while he let the current have its way with him. He sucked in great mouthfuls of air whenever he could, and he swallowed more than a little water. But he was being carried away from those guns on the bridge.

Yet this was only trading peril for peril; a man couldn't live long at the mercy of this stream, and he tried feebly to make it to one of the dark shores. It was like pitting himself against a mountain wall—a wall that moved and had a mind of its own—but at last some vagary of the current swept him toward the western bank, thrusting him hard against a boulder. He had enough consciousness left to wrap his arms tightly around the rock, and here he clung until a measure of strength came back to him. Now he found that his feet touched bottom, but for a long time he was content to remain where he was.

Overhanging bushes shadowed him, almost brushing his face, and he grasped at them experimentally with one hand. Then he became aware that somebody was threshing through the underbrush nearby, and he turned rigid, scarcely daring to breathe. Through the interlacing leaves and branches, he made out a bulky figure, stooped low in frantic search; and from afar came a voice, faint with distance and almost lost beneath the creek's roar.

"Any sign of him?" the voice called.

The searcher straightened, cupping his hands to his mouth. "It's like looking for a needle in a haystack. He might be a mile downstream by now!"

The other voice shouted again from the vicinity of the bridge, but the sound didn't quite carry to Chip. The one who'd been doing the searching must have heard, though, for he turned back then and soon lost himself from Chip's view. But still Chip clung to the rock, waiting many minutes before he dragged himself to the bank.

He'd hoped that his try at escaping might have so disconcerted Sheriff Frank Busby and his deputies that Singin' Sam and Clark Rayburn would also have been able to make a getaway in the ensuing confusion. But only one man had come to search the creek bank, and that meant that Busby had sagely stayed where he could keep a watchful eye on his remaining prisoners. And shortly a more thorough search would doubtless be made for Chip Halliday.

That last thought sent Chip stumbling away from the creek, and he came out of the fringing willows and into a broken land of coulees and ridges. From the higher rises he saw that he was just a little south of Tumblerock town. His teeth were chattering and his clothes clung wetly to him, but he put his will against the temptation to try and build a fire, warming himself instead by walking as briskly as he could.

Soon the chill was out of him, and his need was for a plan of action. He thought of Hope Brennan and wished fervently that she'd stay clear of Tumblerock and possible capture. Singin' Sam and Clark Rayburn would be lodged in jail, of course, and after an hour he ventured into the town, approaching it from the southwest and crawling furtively toward that weedy lot next to the jail-building where he'd once found Tate Strunk awaiting him.

From this vantage point, the jail looked dark and deserted, but he couldn't see the front of the building, and there might be a light in Busby's office. Probably the sheriff was out searching the creek bank, but then again, Busby might have put others at that task. Chip was edging nearer to the jail when from within its interior a squeaky, tuneless voice raised itself in song:

> *The old oak-en-n-n bucket; the iron-bound*
> *buck-et-t-t,*
> *The moss-covered buck-et, that hung in the*
> *well-l-l-l . . .*

Chip eased closer to one of the barred windows. "Sam——?" he called softly.

The song trailed away, and a moment later McAllister's old face was pressed against the bars. "Chip, you loco son-of-a-gun!" Sam cried gleefully. "So you made it! Them bullets had me worried, and that crick didn't look like anything to give a man pleasure!"

"Rayburn is there with you?"

"Here, Halliday," the Forlorn leader said, his sad face appearing beside McAllister's.

"How are things shaping? You two been officially charged with anything?"

"They'll hold a coroner's inquest into the death of St. John tomorrow," Rayburn said. "I'm being held for that. If the evidence stacks up right, I'll be charged with St. John's murder and ordered held for trial. And Alessandro will see that the evidence is what he wants it to be. I knew it would come to this someday. I've outlived my usefulness to him, so he's bent on destroying me."

Singin' Sam said, "I'm still an escaped convict, I guess. The sheriff ain't wasted much time on me."

"What about Busby?" Chip asked Rayburn. "Does he belong to Alessandro like everybody else around here?"

"I've never been sure," Rayburn said. "Alessandro's weight can swing a lot of votes, and Busby likely never forgets that. But mostly I think it's just plain stupidity that makes him Alessandro's tool. How Busby would act if a real showdown shaped, I don't know."

Singin' Sam said, "You reckon we ought to tip our hand, Chip, and tell that tin-toter who you and me really are?"

Chip shook his head. "We haven't any proof we can lay our hands on in a minute," he said. "Besides, there's something else I'm after now. The scalp of Scton Alessandro. The governor wants to make law-abiding country out of the Tumblerocks, but he'll never have it till Alessandro's salted down. And I figure that Alessandro, given enough rope, will hang himself. The town's quiet; there's no lynching shaping up, so I reckon Alessandro's next move will be at the inquest. I took that dive off the bridge because I figured the jail would be a deathtrap, but now I'm thinking you're as safe here tonight as you'd be any place. And I won't be far away."

Rayburn said, "You've got to believe me, Halliday; I had no hand in whatever happened to Justin St. John."

"Sheriff's comin' down the corridor!" Singin' Sam hissed and instantly began singing again:

> *The old oak-en-n-n bucket, the iron-bound*
> * buck-et-t-t,*
> *Th' moss-covered buck-et, that hung in the*
> * well-l-l-l . . .*

With that unmelodious rendition ringing in his ears, Chip scurried away into the deeper shadows and here he paused, listening to Sam's squeaky singing until the words sang into his consciousness and tied themselves to some nebulous memory. And suddenly Chip was quivering with excitement, for he was recalling something that might tangle Seton Alessandro's twine, and the need to substantiate his newborn theory became like a hunger.

There were a few things he must know first, and Clark Rayburn could probably give him the information. But Singin' Sam was into another stanza of his song, and by this token Chip recognized a signal that the sheriff was still in the offing. So Chip cat-footed out of this weedy lot and to the boardwalk of Tumblerock's main street. With a bold and appraising eye, he studied the horses lined at the nearest hitchrail, selected the one that looked the speediest, stepped up into its saddle and lined off into the night . . .

This was the hour of the coroner's inquest, and the gathering place was a large and barnlike building, weathered by the winds and rains of many years and made old by constant usage. It sat at almost the precise center of Tumblerock's false-fronted main street, and sometimes it was a dance hall, but often it was a council chambers. The nooning sun made an oven of it, and its benches were crowded by sweating townsmen while others strewed the aisles and crammed up against the walls. Its ceiling was low and its windows were high, and the air was stifling.

On a raised platform at the mammoth room's far end—a platform where musicians stationed themselves when a dance was held—a row of chairs had been placed, six of them against the wall with a seventh to one side of the front of the platform. A jury of perspiring townsmen occupied the six chairs; Jasper Fogg was perched precariously on the seventh. He had put himself in charge of this inquest; no one had challenged him, and at the appointed hour he clapped his hands for order.

"Fellow citizens, we are gathered here to hold a coroner's inquest," he announced in his most pompous oratorical manner. "In the absence of Doc Swanstrom, I've been requested to fill his official place. We are all agreed, I'm sure, that no medico is required to certify that the deceased in question came to his untimely end as a result of a gunshot. His body was found the day before yesterday by Sheriff Busby, and the deceased has been identified as a certain Justin St. John."

Turning to the six jurymen, he said, "All you gentlemen have seen the body?"

There was a general nod, and Sheriff Busby was called to testify. The burly lawman was seated near the front of the room, Clark Rayburn beside him, his face rigid. Quite a scattering of deputies was posted near the sheriff, and they gave their strict attention to Rayburn while the sheriff was sworn in. With colorless words Busby described finding the body in a clump of bushes near the Bear Creek schoolhouse, and at the finish Fogg mopped his pink face and said, "We really need Doc Swanstrom for an official opinion on the next question, but I imagine you've seen enough dead men in your time, Sheriff, to give a qualified answer. How long would you say St. John had been dead when you found him?"

"About two days," Busby judged.

"Hm-m-m," Fogg reflected. "That would make it about the night of the big storm. I understand there are some other witnesses—a couple of men who gave you some information after they'd heard of your discovery of the body."

"Right here," Busby said, and two range-garbed men stood up. Fogg said, "We'll take you one at a time. You there, come to the stand and have yourself sworn in."

When the rite was performed, Fogg said, "Your name?"

The man squinted one eye and spat a stream of tobacco juice from the corner of his mouth. "You damn well know my name," he said.

Fogg frowned. "This is for the records and must be done in the proper way. Yes, I know you, Piute. You are employed at Seton Alessandro's ranch?"

"You know that too, Fogg," Piute said.

"Let's have your story."

"There ain't much to it. The night of the big rain, me and Cultus, there, was in the saddle when the storm blew up. We headed for the home ranch mighty fast, but we could see we was in for a wetting before we got there. So Cultus up and opined that it might be smart to get the roof of the Bear Creek schoolhouse over our heads."

"And you went to the schoolhouse?"

"We got there, but we didn't go inside. By then it was deep dark, but there was a light in the teacherage; and we could see inside. Three people were palavering—the school-marm, Clark Rayburn, and another jigger, a stranger. Rayburn and this jigger was doing some tall arguing; I could see the stranger shaking his fist under Rayburn's nose. Then Rayburn cuffed the other gent hard, slamming him out of my sight."

"You're sure it was Rayburn you saw?"

"Dead sure!" said Piute.

"What did you do then?"

"The setup had the look of a fair-enough scrap, one man against another, and it was no skin off our noses. We decided we might just as well chance the rain as get mixed up in a fracas that was somebody else's business."

"And the man Rayburn was quarreling with; this stranger? You've seen him since?"

"He's over at the furniture store right now, filling a coffin," Piute said. "We had a look at him out of curiosity when we loped into town and heard about the sheriff finding a body. It was the same man, I'll swear to that."

All this while Clark Rayburn sat with his eyes ahead, no expression crossing his face, no words of denial bursting from him. A mighty buzz of talk was sweeping the room, but Rayburn seemed unconscious of it, and of the eyes that were now turned upon him. He remained just as wooden while the second man, Cultus, was sworn in and told virtually the same story as Piute. After that Fogg raised his hands, commanding silence, and in the heavy hush of it said, "What have you got to say about this, Rayburn?"

"Why isn't Seton Alessandro here?" Rayburn asked.

Fogg frowned. "This matter is no concern of Mr. Alessandro's, and he's too busy to trifle with every inquest that comes along. Are you trying to cloud the issue, Rayburn?"

The Forlorn leader came to his feet then. In a toneless voice he said, "You've staged as nice a farce as I'll likely ever witness, Fogg. You'd like me to contribute to the show by making a vehement denial of this pack of lies Alessandro's men have just told. I'll not accommodate you. Yes, I was at the Bear Creek schoolhouse the night of the storm. But no stranger was there at the same time. I think you know that, Fogg. And you can tell Seton Alessandro that his frame-up is airtight!"

The thing in Jasper Fogg's eyes might have been a mute appeal. "I'd hoped you'd say something more to your own defense, Rayburn," he said. He coughed then, and colored slightly. Turning to the jury he said, "I've slips of paper here which I'll pass out for your verdict. You can withdraw for discussion if you'd like. Under the circumstances, you'll have to render one of two verdicts: either Justin St. John died at the hands of a party or parties unknown, or he died at the hands of Clark Rayburn. In the latter case, your verdict will be construed as a recommendation that Rayburn be held for trial."

The slips passed around, the jury shuffled its feet restlessly, chewed at pencils and whispered among itself. One by one the slips were returned to Fogg, and each was examined. Four bore a verdict against Rayburn; two named parties unknown as the cause of Justin St. John's death.

For a moment Jasper Fogg stood holding these slips, oblivious to the fact that every eye was on him, every man in this room awaiting his pronouncement. For it had come to Fogg how easily he might twist these results if he chose; even the jury itself did not know how it had collectively voted. He'd liked no part of this day's work, had Fogg; it was another of those deals for Alessandro that wouldn't stand the light of day. Yet he could say that the majority of the votes stood in favor of a parties unknown verdict; he could do that, and no one would be the wiser.

Clearing his throat, he said, "Sheriff, the verdict is in. You'll return Clark Rayburn to your jail and hold him for trial."

Thus the inquest ended, and thus Jasper Fogg had his one chance at partial redemption and threw that chance away. In a sense he too had stood on trial; he had faced the tribunal of his own conscience, and the judgment had gone against him.

14 : The Trap Is Set

For an hour Seton Alessandro had sat in Jasper Fogg's cubbyhole of an office on Tumblerock's main street, and that hour had filled him with an impatience that had become almost agony. The swivel chair was hard and apparently designed to break a man's back; the room itself was stifling, and Alessandro wished now that he'd waited in his cool town house on the crest above. Taking a short turn about the room, he wondered if he could show himself at the inquest and see how the proceedings were coming; but when he stepped to the office doorway, he saw the big dancehall disgorging the crowd. With a sigh, Alessandro went back to the chair.

Fogg was slow in coming. At last the lawyer shuffled into the office, plopped upon a straight-backed chair and mopped his round, pink face with a handkerchief. His string tie was askew, his baggy, black suit looked as though he'd slept in it, and the lawyer himself had a beaten, jaded air about him. Alessandro frowned and said, "Well——?"

"It's over, Seton," Fogg announced. "Piute and that other cutthroat spoke their pieces like proper Poll-parrots. It did the trick. Rayburn's being held for trial."

"How did Rayburn take it?"

"He asked about you, and he made a little speech," Fogg said, and proceeded to relate it.

A great, good humor began to take the stiffness out of Alessandro, and he said, "Fine, Fogg. Fine. You're a good man at your work when you put your mind to it. Now I've got Rayburn where I want him!"

"I'm damned if I see how," Fogg countered, a sharp note of exasperation in his voice. "This affair is bound to come to the attention of Helena, especially when Rayburn goes on trial for killing the governor's man. Perjured witnesses will hang Rayburn; but the other Forlorners will still be pardoned, and you'll have lost in the long run, Seton. Is the satisfaction you'll get out of destroying Rayburn worth that?"

Alessandro said, "My luck's running high again. Look out there on the street, Fogg, and see who's ridden into town. Hail him over here, will you?"

Across the way, Tate Strunk was just swinging from a saddle, his thick shoulders sagging with weariness. From the doorway Fogg called softly and beckoned with a quick gesture of one pudgy hand. When the prison guard came across the street and framed himself in the entrance to the office, Alessandro said, "Where the devil have you been keeping yourself the last couple of days?"

Frustration had put Strunk in a bitter frame of mind; the proof of it was in the tightness of his mouth. "I tangled my twine somehow," he confessed. "That first night, I waited below the pass into Forlorn, sure that Halliday and McAllister would come by. But the only thing that moved along the trail was a freight wagon. Since then, I've been riding in circles, looking for a sign. I've seen enough hill country to do me a lifetime. I tell you, those two have vanished as completely as a lot of others who headed into these damn Tumblerocks."

Alessandro smiled faintly. "It may interest you to know

that the freight wagon you let pass by you was carrying your flown birds. But never mind. Things have happened while you've been holding communion with nature, Strunk. Sam McAllister is back in the Tumblerock jail, and Clark Rayburn is locked up with him—charged with the murder of Justin St. John."

That spread a show of surprise across Strunk's face. "I don't get it," he said. "What's happened?"

"The details aren't important," Alessandro said. "There's a new job for you, Strunk—a bigger and better job with pay that will put you on plush. Are you interested?"

Strunk said, "Keep on talking, mister!"

"Rayburn and McAllister will be in separate cells tonight. I'll talk to Sheriff Busby and arrange that. By dusk, Busby will be busy elsewhere. You will go into the jail, help yourself to the keys and let Rayburn out of his cell, Strunk. Tell him any kind of story that suits your fancy; he doesn't know you, and he probably won't look a gift horse too closely in the mouth. You might say that you ran into that schoolteacher, Hope Brennan, and she bribed you into freeing Rayburn. She happens to be his daughter. In any case, you get him out of jail."

Strunk nodded slowly. "And then——?"

"Head him toward Forlorn and ride far enough along with him to make sure he goes back to the valley."

"What about McAllister?"

"He isn't so important now; once I wanted him dead so that he wouldn't give a certain piece of information to Rayburn. But perhaps he's already done that. Then again, perhaps he hasn't. I have it! After you've freed Rayburn and started him north, slip back to the jail. Shooting McAllister will be like spearing a fish in a rain barrel. "It's too cheap a chance to throw away."

Strunk said, "I understand." Hesitation tied his tongue for a moment, then he added, "You spoke of a good payoff for a job this size."

Alessandro dipped into a pocket, produced a roll of currency and tossed it to Strunk without examining it. "Get out of here now," Alessandro said. "I don't want people seeing us together."

Strunk gone, Alessandro smiled at Fogg. "Now do you grasp the idea?" he said. "I'd planned to use Piute for the job, but Strunk makes a better man, seeing as Rayburn knows Piute and would be suspicious. Besides, if anything goes wrong, there's no connection between Strunk and myself. But nothing must go wrong. Rayburn returns to the valley an outlaw; after his taste of the inquest, he'll know he'd stand no chance at the trial. If he's sensible, he stays holed up in the valley, and if the governor tries to root him out, I'm banking that the Forlorners will protect him. Our little outlaw sanctuary stays outlaw, Fogg."

Jasper Fogg had the nauseated look of a man who'd tasted a bitter brew. "I think," he said slowly, "that I shall get very drunk today."

Alessandro let him shuffle out of the office, then smiled to himself, a man who'd moved his pawns to their proper places on the board and had only to wait now for the inevitable completion of a carefully calculated play. He came to a stand, ready to leave for his house on the hill. But Piute stepped quietly into the office, making a display of his yellowish teeth in a caricature of a smile. "Howdy, boss," he said. "I'm heading out to the ranch now."

Alessandro nodded. "Fogg tells me you did a good job at the inquest."

"I've been thinking about that," Piute said. "Perjury carries a stiff stretch in stony lonesome—even perjury at an inquest. Sometimes a man is asked to do queer things for the pay he gets."

Alessandro said, "I know. I know. You've got a bonus coming." He felt in his pocket and remembered the roll he'd given Strunk. "I've no money with me now."

"Not even a little for the time being?"

Frowning, Alessandro knelt before Fogg's safe and spun the dial. "Wait a minute," he said.

There was a sheaf of currency inside the safe; Alessandro counted off some bills and passed them to Piute. The new foreman's boots were beating a departure down the board-walk when Alessandro thrust the rest of the money back into the safe, but in doing so he dislodged a pile of papers which spilled to the floor. Gathering them, Alessandro was restoring the papers to their former place when he noticed the thick envelope which bore the name of the governor of Montana.

Swinging the safe's door shut, Alessandro came erect, that letter in his hand. His thin lips were drawn to a taut line as he slipped his thumb under the flap of the envelope. . . .

To Colorado Jack Ives, the two nights and a day he'd been imprisoned in Seton Alessandro's ranch house had seemed endless, a confinement beyond bearing. Only that interlude of last evening when Alessandro had had him and Lia fetched to the study had broken the monotony, but since then Ives had paced with fear as well as anger. Now he was well into his second day, and the hour had come when he must make his try at escape.

Somewhere on this second floor was Lia, perhaps just beyond the wall in the next room. At times he'd heard her pounding frantically at her door, but he'd never been exactly sure where she was located. Also he'd heard the faint stir-rings of a sentry in the hallway often enough, but today there was no sound in the upper house. And today Colorado Jack was going to make his play.

That interview with Alessandro had whetted his despera-tion and put a gnawing fear in him, not so much for himself as for Lia. The dark-eyed girl knew something about Ales-sandro—some secret that had to do with Justin St. John, who'd been sent to the Tumblerocks by the governor. The day that she'd persuaded Colorado to flee the range with her she'd intimated that she held a club over Alessandro's head, and when they'd been captured in the far northern reaches of Bear Creek Basin, she'd flung St. John's name in Alessandro's face. And last night she'd threatened to find a way to tell who had really killed St. John. That had been a mistake. Ives had seen the fear crawl into Alessandro's eyes as the man had ordered his prisoners returned upstairs. And Ives had known that Lia had doomed herself at that moment. A secret that menaced Seton Alessandro also menaced its possessor.

That was why Colorado Jack had to escape at any cost, and now he had fashioned a way. Long ago he'd explored this prison room thoroughly, only to realize that it offered scant opportunities in the way of escape. Its heavy door stayed locked, and usually a guard paced beyond the door. The one window faced north and was unbarred, but therein lay the devilish cleverness of those who'd placed him here. From this window he could see the barn and corrals of the ranch, and, between them, a sweeping stretch of the basin. But he could also see down below, into the picket-fenced enclosure where Alessandro's hunting hounds snarled and bickered among themselves.

No pedigreed pack this, but the product of strange matings, these huge, savage dogs barred the way to freedom more effectively than steel or locks or stone could do. Some among Alessandro's crew had a way with the hounds—savagery calling to savagery perhaps—but Colorado Jack was not one of these. He would have faced a gun without flinching; he would have dared myriad dangers, but there was something about Alessandro's hounds that had always raised the hackles on his neck and filled him with a watery weakness.

Usually well fed, the hounds had been given nothing to eat these past two days. This Colorado knew, for he'd watched the pen often and he'd seen the brutes grow more savage with the passing hours. And from this observation had grown his idea.

Five meals had been served to Ives since he'd been imprisoned here; the tray from the noon meal still stood on a table near the door. There'd been beefsteak and fried potatoes at three of those meals, and the beefsteak, carefully saved, was now in Colorado's pocket. This was his key to freedom if luck was with him, and now that he was ready, he hoisted the sash of the window, listened for a moment to see if anyone stirred in the hall, then tossed his leg over the sill. A rain pipe ran down the side of the building; he reached it by stretching an arm, got as good a hold as possible and swung his weight to the pipe, fearful for a moment that it would not sustain him.

Below, the hounds were already eyeing him, growling deep in their throats. Lowering himself slowly, he saw them begin to converge beneath him, and he reached for a piece of steak and tossed it awkwardly. There was a snarling rush for the meat.

Ives dropped to the ground then; his palms were moist with sweat, and he felt big and clumsy and inadequate to the task ahead. His impulse was to make a frantic run for the picket fence, but he fought against the urge and began a slow walk instead. The enclosure was only fifty feet wide, and from where he'd landed there was but half the distance to cover. But two of the hounds were stalking stiff-legged toward him, growling and baring their fangs. Tossing a second piece of steak, Ives reached the fence in a single bound and lunged upward for a hold on the pickets.

He failed at the first try, leaped again, felt his fingers close over the pickets. Something snapped at one of his bootheels as he hauled himself upward. His scalp tingling, his mouth dry, he perched atop the fence and hurled his last piece of beefsteak. He'd reached safety, but a commotion among the hounds might fetch a guard, and he didn't want that. Looking up, he glimpsed Lia; she was in another of those rooms facing northward, and he waved to her reassuringly and saw the flutter of her fingers in reply. Then he dropped to the catwalk that abutted the outer fence, and from there to the ground.

For a moment he paused, panting hard, his heart pounding furiously. Then he began a cautious circling of the house. At the front door a man lounged on guard. Colorado knew that man; he had a reputation for ruthlessness that made him adequate to his task, and Ives backed away, setting off at an angle that kept the house between himself and the guard. Under different circumstances he'd have chanced rushing the guard, gun and all, but since he himself was weaponless, the odds were too great. He had to remember that Lia was still locked above.

That made his first need a gun. Away from the ranch and sheltered by trees, he struck off toward Tumblerock on foot, keeping to cover and remembering that any of Alessandro's riders might be in the vicinity. He told himself that he'd be back before nightfall; he promised that Lia would be out of that house soon, but he knew that his play had to be foolproof so long as her life was at stake.

Such was the run of his thoughts as he covered the first mile to the south of Alessandro's ranch. And then, as he strode through a clump of trees, he saw a rider briefly skylined ahead before the man dipped over a rise. Instantly Ives was pressing himself against the trunk of a giant cottonwood whose branches overhung the trail. And instantly he was formulating a plan of action.

That oncoming rider was going to pass along this very trail, and likely that man carried a gun. That made the menace and the objective one and the same, and Ives shinnied up the tree as quietly as he could, wormed out upon the biggest branch above the trail and got himself into position for a quick drop upon the man who would pass below.

He was this way, poised and ready, when Chip Halliday came riding down the trail.

15 : Lia Talks

Chip Halliday, riding out of Tumblerock on a stolen horse, had had Alessandro's ranch as his destination, but when the town had fallen far behind, an impulse veered his course to the northeast. The night had turned magic with moonlight since he'd left Singin' Sam and Clark Rayburn at the jail, and he had no trouble recognizing landmarks. More familiar with this country than he'd been that storm-swept night he'd ridden into it, he came almost unerringly to the Bear Creek schoolhouse.

The building was dark and deserted, of course, but using it as a starting point Chip began circling, making no effort at silence and sometimes calling Hope's name aloud. But the better part of an hour passed before he heard a rustling in the brush, and Hope stepped into a moon-dabbled clearing. Out of the saddle, he took a step toward her and she was into his arms at once, her heart pounding against his.

"Dad——?" she cried. "And Singin' Sam?"

"In jail," he replied and told her of the capture and his own escape. "I supposed you'd hang around, hoping we'd show back," he concluded.

"I saw Busby take all of you toward town," she said. "At

first I was going to follow, but I was afraid that might not be so wise. I've staked out my horse yonder in the brush, intending to hide out here till morning at least. But what now, Chip? Are you leaving dad and Singin' Sam in jail?"

"I could get them out, of course," he said. "I could even wire the governor, if needs be. But your dad would still have to stand trial for the murder of St. John. I've a hunch that things will be different in a few more hours. Tell me, Hope, has Alessandro got a wife or daughter?"

She shook her head. "There's a girl who lives with him, though. She's called Lia Alessandro, and she's his niece, I believe. She's about my age. Why, Chip?"

"Hmmm," he mused, ignoring her question. "You've seen Alessandro's ranch, I suppose. Tell me about it—everything you can remember."

Puzzlement in her eyes, she began painting a word picture of the place; he listened attentively, then put his foot into a stirrup. "Climb up behind me," he said when he'd swung into the saddle. "We're riding."

She obeyed, and with her arms around him he went jogging back to the schoolhouse. Here he dismounted, tried the gate leading into the teacherage yard, stepped through it and had a look around, heading first one direction and then another. "Got any matches?" he asked. "Mine were doused in Bear Creek." When she handed him some, he lighted several for a better look. "You know, I've never really seen this place," he said. "I was only in this yard that stormy night and in the dark before the next dawn."

Hope said, "Do you delight in arousing my curiosity? Or maybe you're just as baffled by what you're doing as I am."

He grinned. "I'm the original sagebrush sleuth tonight," he said. "Give me a hair out of the tail of a curly wolf and I'll tell you how much the varmint weighs and how he spends his evenings. Now I need a look at Alessandro's ranch. But tomorrow will be the time for that. If I'm not mistaken, Senor Alessandro will be attending the inquest, and maybe most of his crew will likewise be in town. A perfect time for a visit. Let's get back to where you left your horse and snatch some beauty sleep."

She bristled with questions, but he found it fun to keep silent. More than that, he wasn't yet sure of himself; and he had no intention of arousing her hope on the strength of a half-formed hunch that had yet to be proved. Spreading his saddle blanket near hers, he was quickly asleep, but the sun was perched almost on top of the pines when he awoke.

They breakfasted on food Hope had gotten from the teacherage the night before, and when he'd saddled again, she put gear on her own mount and looked at him expectantly. But Chip said, "I want you to stay here, Hope. And when night comes, head back to Forlorn Valley. You can find that stairway to the sky, can't you?"

"I can find it," she said. "But there's danger at Alessandro's ranch, and you're going there."

"All the more reason why I must go alone," he said soberly. Taking her by the elbows, he looked at her intently. "Your dad's going to be safe," he said. "I think I can just about promise you he'll be free by nightfall. But that depends on my luck today, and the job can be done better alone. We've all got to have a meeting place afterward, and Forlorn Valley's the safest spot. Will you do as I wish, Hope?"

He thought he'd have an argument on his hands, but she said, "Very well, Chip. If you think it's best." He kissed her then, gently, and stepped up into his saddle. "Good girl!" he said and waved his hand and went riding on through the timber.

Thus he took the trail to Alessandro's ranch, and as the miles unreeled he kept a watch for other riders; he'd not forgotten that Sheriff Busby might have a posse out scouring the country for him. He was gambling that the excitement of the inquest in town today would claim those who might otherwise be in saddles; and the passing minutes proved him right, for he came across a silent, deserted land. When he got a glimpse of the buildings of Alessandro's ranch, he realized he'd veered too far south, and he turned and faced northward, riding boldly along.

The country was more open than it had been in the vicinity of the schoolhouse, but there were many of those park-like glades, and he found another clump of trees just ahead of him. He saw it from a rise, dipped down out of sight, climbed another rise and came down atilt into the trees. For an instant his eyes were at a level with branches which would be above him when he reached the trees, and in that instant he had a partial glimpse of a man sprawled out upon the limb of a giant cottonwood.

His eyes narrowing, Chip's first impulse was to leave the trail and circle around that tree, but he continued onward instead as a new plan of action came to him. He'd been walking his horse, and he kept the mount at that same pace, but when he was almost under the cottonwood he suddenly jabbed hard with his spurs, an action that sent the horse bolting forward. Thus Ives, timed to the pace of the oncoming rider, dropped from the limb to find nobody beneath him. At the same time Chip was hauling hard on the reins. Swinging his horse about, he dived from the saddle, full upon Ives, and the two of them, locked together, threshed about the trail.

It was a short fight. That fall to the hard-packed earth had shaken most of the strength out of Ives; Chip could tell that at once. He got his man beneath him, pinned Ives's shoulders under his knees and said, "Are you ready to holler 'Uncle'? Or do I have to choke the stuffings out of you?"

"Your hand, mister!" Ives gasped weakly, and Chip came to his feet, his left fist cocked and ready. A glance showed him that Ives was unarmed; and that made them even, for Chip had been without a gun since he'd handed his to Singin' Sam in Clark Rayburn's cabin in Forlorn Valley. Chip wished now that he'd thought to get that .38 that Hope kept in the teacherage, for Ives had a wiry look about him and the man's breath was coming back fast.

Weaponless, Chip was also bareheaded; his sombrero had gone sailing down Bear Creek the night before. Ives looked at him long and intently, astonishment widening his eyes, and then he said, "They give those kind of haircuts in stony lonesome! You sure ain't Singin' Sam McAllister, so that makes you Chip Halliday!"

Chip nodded. "And you?"

"Ives. Colorado Jack Ives."

Chip remembered that name; Hope Brennan had mentioned it once. "Alessandro's foreman," Chip said.

"Not anymore," Ives retorted with a show of temper. "Man, Alessandro's no friend of mine. Nor of yours, either. You've got to believe that!"

"It sounds pretty," Chip said. "But how much truth is there to it?"

"Look," Ives countered. "I have no gun. That's why I was laying for you; I wanted yours. Would I be climbing trees a hoot and a holler from my own ranch to get a gun if I was on good terms with Alessandro?"

"No," Chip agreed. "You wouldn't. Talk, mister. I'll listen."

Whereupon Colorado Jack Ives unfolded his tale, and it began with his love for Lia Alessandro and the developments that had ensued since Chip Halliday had come riding into the Tumblerock country. He spoke of the alliance between Tate Strunk and Alessandro; told of the talk that Lia had overheard between those two, and of Lia's determination to run away from Alessandro and their subsequent capture. At the finish Ives said, "But when Alessandro grabbed us, we were trying to cut sign on you and McAllister. We were out to warn you against that devil!"

A man impressed, Chip was fitting the pieces together. Now he knew why Tate Strunk had so persistently clung to his trail since the escape from Deer Lodge. And the whole pattern of Alessandro's scheming was becoming clear at last. The man's need to keep Forlorn Valley an outlaw haven had a dollar-and-cents basis, and the extent to which Alessandro would go to keep the situation unchanged was also obvious. And because everything Ives had said fitted into the theory that Hope had formed about Alessandro when Chip had arrested Clark Rayburn in Forlorn, Chip sensed that Ives was telling the truth.

"So Lia Alessandro's under lock and key at the ranch," Chip mused. "Well, mister, you want her out of there, and so do I. Shall we get at it?"

The bleakness of Ives's weathered face broke as he grinned. *"Muy pronto!"* he said.

Leading Chip's horse, they started down the trail, Ives explaining about the man on guard as they walked. Ground-anchoring the horse among the trees, Chip mapped a piece of strategy that sent the two of them cat-footing forward in different directions, each keeping to cover and moving upon the ranch house from an opposite side. Chip had lost sight of Ives as he crawled on hands and knees around a corner of the house to within twenty feet of the sentry. Now Chip stood poised and ready, and he was this way when Ives stepped boldly into sight at the far corner of the house and called, "Hey, Yampa!"

That brought the sentry whirling around, his jaw falling and his hand sweeping toward his holstered gun. But at that instant while Ives was chaining the man's astonished attention, Chip darted forward in a wild, lunging dive that hurled him upon the sentry and bore the man to the ground. The fellow's gun exploded, but the man had gotten it tangled in his holster. Grasping the sentry by the shirtfront, Chip hauled him erect, measured the distance to the man's stubbled jaw and let go with a left that dropped the man again, his eyes rolling upward.

"Out!" Chip panted and blew upon his bruised knuckles. Ives, coming forward, began stripping the bullet-studded belt from the man's middle. "At least we've got ourselves a gun," he observed. "There may be another jigger on watch inside the house. I couldn't tell for sure before I left. But likely not; otherwise the gunshot would have fetched him."

"I'll go after the girl," Chip said. "You stay here and keep an eye peeled. If this fellow starts coming awake, tap him on the head. Or dump him into yonder well and cool him off, if it isn't too deep."

Ives was all eagerness now; patently he would have preferred to go into the house to Lia's rescue, but he could see the need for a man to stay on guard for he didn't protest. Chip said, "You keep the gun. Fire it as a signal if anybody comes loping."

Shouldering into the house, he threaded the hallway and climbed to the second story. There was no one on guard, and he called softly, "Lia . . . ? Miss Alessandro . . . ?" and there was a hubbub at one of the doors studding this hall.

"Who is it?" Lia cried. "I heard a shot——!"

Beside the door a key hung on a nail, obviously for the convenience of whoever brought food to the girl. Chip unlocked the door and let himself into the room, but he closed the door then and put his back to it, watching the swift play of emotion that crossed the face of this dark and exotic girl as she saw him.

"I'm Chip Halliday," he said. "You've seen me before, haven't you?"

Her hand fluttered to her throat, her dark eyes growing wider, and Chip said, "I came here the night of the storm—remember? I rode up to your gate, got through it, and bumped up against that well out in the yard. I'd almost forgotten about the well until I heard a man sing *The Old Oaken Bucket.* Strange how important the little things can sometimes be. I was almost out on my feet, that night, but I stayed alive long enough to see you come out of this house—you and Seton Alessandro carrying the body of Justin St. John between you. Then I passed out."

He thought she was going to scream; her eyes grew even wider, but she said in a small and shaky voice, "That's true!"

"You must have loaded me back onto my horse," he said. "You moved me to the Bear Creek schoolhouse and dumped me in its yard. Up until last night, it never occurred to me that the place where I went unconscious and the place where I recovered might have been miles apart. And Alessandro left St. John's body nearby, too—left it where suspicion would be pointed at Clark Rayburn when the body was found, seeing as Rayburn was at the schoolhouse that night. Is that right?"

She nodded, and Chip said in a gentler voice, "Don't be afraid, girl. I'm here to get you out of this hellhole. Come on. Colorado Jack is waiting for us below."

Taking her by the wrist, he led her down the stairs and out of the house. The tenseness left Ives as they appeared, and Lia was instantly into his arms. Smiling, Chip said, "That'll have to wait until we've more time, folks. Me, I'll breathe easier when this place is behind us."

"That's right," Ives agreed. "And the first thing we need is horses. Wait here and I'll throw gear on three of Alessandro's saddlers, Halliday; you might as well leave your horse and take a fresh mount. But you keep a watch to the south meanwhile. I won't be able to see the trail from town from behind the house, but I'll keep an eye peeled to the north while I'm saddling. If any of the boys should come down out of the basin, I'll see 'em first."

"A good plan," Chip judged. "Get at it, and make it fast." Ives instantly started around the house, and Lia would have followed him, but Chip seized her wrist again. "There's a lot I want to hear from you. A good man's neck is in danger of getting stretched by a hangman's rope, and the sooner I have the whole truth the better. How about it?"

Alessandro's sentry still sprawled nearby; he had not yet begun to groan his way back to consciousness. Lia cast a swift glance at the man, and words came with a rush. "Alessandro killed St. John," she said. "But he didn't mean for me to know. I was out riding that night, and when the rain started I was nearer this ranch than town. So I rode here, and I came in to find St. John dead on the floor of the study and Alessandro standing over him, a smoking gun in his hand."

Chip said, "Something tells me you were mighty close to death yourself at that moment."

"He told me the man was an outlaw who'd come to enter Forlorn Valley and had broken into the ranch house to steal whatever he could. He was terribly agitated; he said it wasn't good for a man in his position to get mixed up in a killing. He said he must move the body far away, and when it was found there'd be no connection between it and him."

"And you believed *that*?" Chip asked dubiously.

"Up until then, he'd given me nothing but kindness," she said. "He was the same to me as a father, and he was in trouble. Yes, I believed him, and I helped carry the body outside. That was when we found you, facedown in the yard. With my help he put you on your horse and tied you there. Then we loaded St. John's body on another horse. And we rode till we came to the schoolhouse. There was a light in the teacherage window, and we could see the schoolteacher and a man inside. The man was Clark Rayburn; I'd seen him before when he came to this ranch on business for the Forlorners."

Chip glanced southward—no sign there of approaching riders. A flurry of sound reached him from the corrals behind the house; that would be Ives roping out the saddlers. Glancing at Lia, Chip said, "And you left me in the schoolhouse yard?"

"He said you'd need help and attention when you recovered and it was best to leave you close to those people."

"I see," Chip said. "The truth is that he didn't dare kill me with you there to witness it. Probably he had no idea, then, who I was, but he wanted me off his ranch in case I'd happened to see too much. So he left me at the schoolhouse, gambling, perhaps, that I'd presume I'd gone unconscious there. I'd see a man and a girl; there was another man and girl in the teacherage. It made a perfect opportunity from Alessandro's viewpoint."

"We hid St. John's body after that, and we rode back to town," Lia went on. "He swore me to secrecy again and again, but I saw the whole truth when I overheard him talking to Tate Strunk a couple of days later. When Strunk told about St. John and insinuated that Alessandro had reason for wanting St. John dead, I knew that St. John had been the man who was killed out here."

"Colorado Jack told me about that talk you overheard," Chip said. "No wonder you wanted to run away from Alessandro when you realized the truth. I suppose Alessandro had been keeping St. John prisoner here; St. John must have made the mistake of sizing up Alessandro as an honest man who had the key to Forlorn Valley. Probably St. John came to Alessandro to ask that devil to get him into the valley with the pardon. Why Alessandro killed him that particular night, we'll probably never know. Perhaps it was because the storm gave Alessandro his chance to remove the body without anyone seeing him. He wasn't counting on you showing up."

She said, *"I hate him!"*

"He's fastened a tight frame on Clark Rayburn," Chip said. "But you're the girl who can bust it wide open. Are you willing to tell a jury the things you've just told me?"

Something in her look gave Chip an inkling of how it had been last evening when Seton Alessandro had humiliated her with his story of her past. She said, "The sooner I face a jury, the better. I'll speak, Mr. Halliday!"

"Good girl!" he said, and glanced around. "It's about time Ives had those saddlers ready. Let's see what's keeping him."

But when they turned the corner of the house, they found themselves confronted by Alessandro's new foreman, Piute, who stood ready and waiting for them, a leveled gun in his hand.

16 : The Hounds of Hate

To Chip, this man before him was a stranger, a hireling of Alessandro's, doubtless, and a formidable one at that, for he could feel Lia stiffening at his side. Chip's own reaction, after the first shock of surprise, was a great bewilderment. He'd kept a careful watch to the south, even as he'd listened to Lia's tale of that storm-swept night, and he'd judged that Colorado Jack, able to see a sweep of basin to the north, had been equally alert. Yet in spite of these precautions, a man was here with a gun and had them trapped neatly.

"Hoist 'em!" Piute ordered.

Raising his hands, Chip said, "Either you've got wings, mister, or you were here all the time."

Piute's laugh revealed his yellowish teeth. "I came riding out from town, and I was down in yonder clump of trees when I heard a shot. That spelled trouble, so I came cat-footing. I saw Yampa down and out, and you and Ives palavering, Halliday. Yeah, I know who you are. I've just been listening to what you and Miss Alessandro had to say to each other."

"Jack?" Lia cried. "You've killed him!"

Piute shook his head. "That would have made too much

noise. I crawled to the back of the house, and I was there when he came around to the corrals. I laid him out with my gun-barrel when he stepped into the saddle shed for gear. Start moving, you two; I want Ives on ice before he wakes up!"

Marched across the yard toward the corrals, Chip and Lia came to the saddle shed with Piute pacing behind them, his gun ready. Colorado Jack sprawled in the open doorway, but he was stirring faintly as the three approached. Piute said, "Get him by the heels, Halliday, and drag him inside. That's fine. Now lift yonder rope down from the wall and hog-tie him. And do a good job of it!"

This little shed had a leathery smell to it; saddles hung from the walls and harness festooned the rafters. With Colorado Jack hauled inside, Chip fell to tying him. Once Lia stepped toward the unconscious man, but a quick gesture of Piute's gun kept her at a distance. Piute stood in the doorway until Ives was tied, then eased forward and tested the rope. A man came lurching across the yard then—the guard, Yampa. Working at his swollen jaw with his fingers, he glared sourly at Chip.

"A helluva guard you turned out to be," Piute observed unsympathetically. "But get another rope and tie up Halliday."

Yampa silently obeyed, and when Chip was also hog-tied, Piute said, "Now take this nightingale back to her cage, Yampa. And when you've locked her up again, squat in the hall and stay there. Alessandro will skin the hide off us if there's another break!"

Yampa went dragging Lia out of the shed, and Piute stood for a moment looking down upon his trussed prisoners. A high good humor in him, he said, "Alessandro should pay a pretty bonus for this job, Halliday. Make yourself comfortable till he gets here."

The door was pulled shut, the beat of Piute's boots faded away, and Chip began threshing about the dusty floor in the semigloom, a man made desperate by the need to escape. He'd come here to test a theory; he'd had a look at the schoolhouse yard last night and there'd been no well. Yet he'd had a nebulous memory of bumping into a well that first night in the Tumblerock country, and he'd found that same well in Alessandro's yard today and sensed the whole truth. He'd gotten Lia out of the house and heard her story, which had confirmed his own suspicions. He'd attained complete success in his mission only to have it snatched from him by the inadvertent arrival of Piute. That one shot Yampa had managed to fire before Chip's fist had put the guard to sleep had blasted Chip's success to pieces. And the finish would come when Alessandro arrived.

Colorado Jack was stirring to consciousness. The man blinked, ran his tongue along his lips, and said weakly, "What the devil happened——?" Chip told him in quick, terse sentences. "Try rolling toward me," he advised. "Maybe we can take a whack at untying each other."

But when they were back to back, they found their efforts futile. Under Piute's gun, Chip had been forced to do a good job of roping Ives, and Yampa had been equally efficient at tying Chip. Both men had their hands trussed behind their backs, but though they could get their fingers on each other's bonds, the knots defied them. Disgusted after an hour of this, Chip rolled away.

"I don't suppose there's a chance that anybody left a knife lying around," he said. "That man of Alessandro's probably took a good look before he left."

"Listen!" Ives cried. "Riders! Sounds like the whole crew's come in. Hear 'em at the corrals?"

But it was something else that suddenly put a singing excitement in Chip. He had come up hard against an object that lay on the floor; his exploring fingers identified it, and he said, "A beer bottle! Somebody had himself a cool drink when he was mending gear. And maybe we've got a ticket out of this place!"

By slow maneuvering, he got the bottle in the vicinity of his feet. His legs were lashed together, but his spurs hadn't been removed, and he hoisted his feet and brought them down hard upon the bottle. But this was a blind effort; he struck the bottle and it went rolling away.

"Bad luck!" he panted, and the heavy breathing of Colorado Jack told him that Ives now shared his excitement. Rolling again, Chip located the bottle and hoisted his feet once more. This time there was the explosion of breaking glass when he brought his boots down. Then Chip was twisting, writhing across the floor, groping with his fingers to get hold on a piece of glass.

He cut himself before he succeeded; he could feel the warm trickle of blood, but his elation made him immune to pain. "Move toward me!" he hissed at Ives, and they were back to back again, and Chip was sawing at Ives's bonds with the jagged edge of the glass. Even then it was a long, arduous process, and time and again Chip paused, his heart pounding frantically and perspiration blinding him, as boots beat close to this saddle shed. But at last Ives said, "That did it!" Sitting up, Colorado Jack began tugging at the knots binding his ankles.

Then Ives was freeing Chip, and the two came to a stand, chasing circulation into their wrists and ankles. A few minutes later they were easing back the door of the shed, and both were astonished to find dusk gathering outside. The bunkhouse was lighted; men were moving between that building and the cookshack, but Chip whistled softly with satisfaction. "A few cayuses standing saddled by the big corral," he observed.

"Lia——?" Ives said and looked toward the house.

"We'll have to come back for her," Chip decided. "We'll run enough risk just getting away from here by ourselves, and we'll do her no good if we die trying to get into the house. Alessandro's game is about over, Ives. Once we get into Tumblerock, we'll see how fast Frank Busby turns his coat when I tell him what Lia told me today. We'll be back here before midnight with the law on our side, even if I have to wire the governor. Come on."

"How do you aim to reach those horses?" Ives asked.

"Like this," Chip said and went stalking boldly across the yard.

Colorado Jack trailed after him. To any casual observer, they might have been two more of the crew, bent upon business of their own. They reached the horses unchallenged, stepped up into saddles and plucked at tie-ropes, but suddenly someone was shouting, "Hey, you two! Stop! *Fellers, it's Ives!*"

The fat was in the fire. Knowing that, Chip tossed aside all pretense, wheeling his horse and spurring it to a gallop. Ives at his side, the two went thundering across the yard, heading for the open reaches beyond the ranch buildings. Guns began an angry banging, boots beat frantically across the ground and saddle leather squealed as men mounted. The chase was on.

Clear of the ranch buildings, Chip would have headed south toward Tumblerock town. But such riders as were already into saddles were fanning out below them, and though Chip tried to swing down the basin, he was forced each time to veer northward instead. This was the twilight hour, neither night nor day, when visibility was poorest, but that was in the fugitives' favor since they made uncertain targets for the hungry guns that harassed them. Chip shouted, "North! It's our only chance!" and he and Ives went galloping in that direction.

Now they were into open country, but ahead of them was one of those many clumps of trees. Chip relished the thought of sheltering timber, but before they reached it his horse faltered, stumbled, made a valiant effort to stay standing, then buckled at the knees, bullet-stricken. Kicking free of the stirrups, Chip lighted running. Instantly Ives was hauling on his reins, extending a hand. "Up here!" he shouted.

Catching at Ives's hand, Chip swung behind the man's saddle, wrapped his arms around Ives, and the timber swallowed them. But once into this shadowy glade, Chip slipped to the ground. "Go on!" he ordered frantically.

Again Ives was hauling at the reins. "Not without you!" he cried. "Climb back up here!"

"This is no time for any damn heroics!" Chip cried. "With that horse double burdened, neither of us will get away. If you want to help me, keep on going and lead them off my trail. It may be a few minutes before they get close enough to find that you're alone. By then I'll be hunkered down in the brush somewhere. My trail leads south, but I can't take it unless you toll 'em off north."

Ives nodded. "You're right!" he decided. "Where do we meet?"

"Can you get past the sentry and into Forlorn?"

"I think so," Ives said. "I've gone in many times as Alessandro's foreman. Possibly the Forlorners don't know I'm not holding that job."

"Then head for the valley," Chip ordered. "If I'm not there by noon tomorrow with Lia, tell the Forlorners to look at the paper Clark Rayburn left in his cabin for them. It's a blanket pardon. And bring the whole bunch of 'em to raid Alessandro's ranch and get Lia if I haven't already done that chore. If you can't budge 'em into action any other way, tell 'em it's an order from the governor's representative."

"OK," Ives said, and went galloping away.

Other hoofs were also beating in this clump of trees. And the pursuit almost upon him, Chip went scurrying into the sheltering shadows. . . .

To the confusion of a ranch gone wild came Seton Alessandro at dusk, dismounting at his own gate to find the yard a milling maelstrom of men and horses. He had spied Piute saddling at one of the corrals and he hurried to his new foreman and got a hold on his elbow. "What's going on?" Alessandro demanded.

Piute told him in as few words as possible, spinning a fast and frantic story. When he'd finished, an ashy pallor had replaced the olive of Alessandro's face, but the man was still capable of a cool and steady judgment.

"You say that some of the boys are already on the trail of Ives and Halliday?"

"Four or five of 'em grabbed whatever horses were ready and waiting," Piute said. "Listen; you can hear 'em shooting up north."

"And Lia's back in her room? And you're sure she managed to tell Halliday everything she knew about St. John?"

"After I'd laid out Ives, I crept to the corner of the house," Piute said. "I heard them talking, and I listened. Lia was spinning a yarn about the night of the storm and how you and her had moved Halliday and St. John's body to the Bear Creek schoolhouse."

Alessandro's thin lips drew tight, and hell was alive in his velvety eyes. "Get out the hounds, Piute," he said. "You're the one man of the crew who can handle them as well as I can. I want the dogs on the trail at once, and I want every rider in his saddle, except Yampa. Spread the boys out; send some of them to the Forlorn pass with orders to let nobody in or out of the valley. But wait! I've got a little deal on that may mean Clark Rayburn will be coming this way tonight. He can go into the valley, but he's not to come out. And some of the other boys must cut off the trail to Tumblerock. There'll be no rest for any man or beast on this ranch till Ives and Halliday are bagged. Do you understand me?"

Piute said, "I reckon I do, boss. It's your neck if they get away."

"They won't get away," Alessandro assured him. "Now jump! I'll be along in a very few minutes."

He went striding toward the house, but he paused near the enclosure that held the hounds, and he studied the upstairs windows for a moment before he went on. Inside the building, he called Yampa, and when the sentry came down from the upstairs hallway, Alessandro was awaiting him in the study.

"Lia's in her room?" Alessandro asked.

Yampa nodded. "I ain't been five feet from the door since I locked her up again."

"The rest of the boys are riding, but you'll stay here, Yampa. From what Piute tells me, you failed me once today. Don't fail me again."

Yampa's eyes narrowed. "She won't get away, boss."

"She'd better not! I'm taking the hounds out of the pen, but I've sized up the back of the house, and she'd break a leg if she tried dropping from the window. Ives must have come down the rain pipe, but she can't reach it from her room. But look in on her once in a while anyway."

"Sure, boss," Yampa said and was dismissed by a wave of Alessandro's hand.

After the man had gone, Alessandro dipped into his pocket and fingered a letter. It was that same letter Jasper Fogg had written to the governor of Montana; Alessandro had read it once, but now he glanced at it again. Then he placed it in the fireplace, touched a match to it and watched till it had burned away. For a space he stood in silent contemplation, then he crossed to his teakwood desk, took his silver-mounted forty-five from a drawer, and also a small vial containing a white, crystalline powder. With a faint smile, he dumped the powder into the wine decanter on his desk.

Then he stepped to the gun case along one wall, fished a key from his pocket and unlocked the case and lifted out a heavy express rifle that had served him in India and Africa. A big game hunter was going on his greatest quest.

Stepping out of the study with the rifle under his arm, he locked the door behind him, called Yampa again and pressed the key into the guard's hand.

"I had business with Jasper Fogg in town today," Alessandro said. "I waited all afternoon in his office for him to return, but he was out getting a skinful and never showed back. So I left a note, telling him to come here as fast as he's able. Probably he'll arrive tonight or tomorrow morning. Let him into the study when he shows up, and tell him to wait there till I return. Understand? *But see that nobody else goes in there!*"

Yampa nodded, and Alessandro went striding out of the house. Behind the fenced enclosure, the hounds, finding the excitement of this night contagious, were snarling and snapping and scratching at the gate. When Alessandro released them, they came swarming out, milling about him and whining eagerly. The hounds were ready, and the hunt was on.

17 : The Trap Is Sprung

The same darkness that had sheltered Chip Halliday and Colorado Jack Ives in their wild dash from Alessandro's ranch had come crowding down upon the Tumblerock jail. The place held only two prisoners tonight, and they now occupied separate cells; Clark Rayburn paced nervously in his, while across the corridor Singin' Sam McAllister hunkered on a hard cot, humming softly as he tried to recall the words of an old ballad having to do with a girl who possessed a wooden leg and a heart of purest gold.

Finally Sam said, "Rest yourself, Rayburn. There's no percentage in wearing out the floor."

Rayburn came to the bars facing upon the corridor and gripped them hard. "Something's shaping up," he said. "First Busby separates us, then he gets out of the building and keeps out. I tell you I've a feeling that a stage has been all set for us. And when the act begins, it won't be to our liking."

"The town's quiet," McAllister observed. "At least there's no lynching in the wind. And Chip said he'd be close by, Rayburn. He's our hole card."

"Listen——!" Rayburn hissed. "Somebody's just come in the front door!"

In the sheriff's office beyond, boots shuffled faintly; whoever prowled the premises was patently making an effort at stealth. Rayburn stiffened, and Singin' Sam felt a flutter at the pit of his stomach. The long day had keyed their nerves to a high pitch, and they were both sharply aware that Alessandro had them at his mercy. That man in the office was obviously bent upon no honest business, and now the prowler loomed in the corridor, weaving unsteadily between the two rows of cells and pausing at last before Rayburn's.

Keys rattled, and the prowler said thickly, "Take these, Rayburn. They were all I could find in Busby's desk. One of them must fit the lock of this cell; another will release McAllister. Now hurry, man!"

Clark Rayburn said coldly, "What sort of trap has Alessandro put you to springing, Fogg?"

Jasper Fogg—for it was the rotund lawyer who stood in the corridor—peered owlishly. "I've horses saddled and waiting for the two of you in the lot next to this building. Get out of here, Rayburn! Get out before another man gets here —a man Alessandro is sending. Don't you understand? I'm double-crossing that devil so I can face myself in the mirror one morning of my life. I've got a strong stomach, but it turned on me today."

He went staggering up the corridor, his boots shuffled in the office again, and Fogg was gone. Rayburn stood staring at the key ring he now held. "Drunk!" Rayburn murmured. "So drunk he could hardly walk!"

"He sure had a skinful," McAllister marveled. "Every saloon in Tumblerock will likely serve drinks at half mast the day that jigger dies! But there's nothing wrong with those keys. Get to work with 'em, Rayburn!"

"It's a trick," Rayburn muttered. "A trick of Alessandro's."

"You're wrong, Rayburn," Sam said. "There may be a

trick shapin' up, but this ain't it. I don't know much about this Fogg gent, but if ever I heard a tortured man talkin', it was him just now. He'd been writhin' down at the bottom of a fiery pit, and the drunker he got today the more he could feel the flames. That's why he got us those keys. Another hour and he may begin losing his nerve, feeling different about what he did. Let's get out of here before he changes his mind and goes crawling to Alessandro."

"Maybe so," Rayburn decided, and fell to experimenting with the keys. "We'll take a whirl at it!"

Time crawled interminably before he found the key that fitted his cell. Then he was across the corridor and fumbling at Singin' Sam's door. When it swung open at last, both men paused, listening, then crept stealthily into Busby's darkened office. Sam whispered, "Let's have a look in the tin-toter's desk. Me, I'd like to have a gun chillin' my belly."

A search of the desk revealed the very guns that had been taken from Rayburn and Sam when they'd been captured near the Bear Creek schoolhouse the night before. Rayburn latched his belt around his lean middle; Sam slipped his gun into the waistband of his pants, and they edged out of the building then and around its corner into that weedy lot where Fogg had said horses would be waiting.

And sure enough, they could see two saddlers back among the thicker shadows, but there was also a man in this lot. He was coming carefully toward the jail, a thick-shouldered, lumpish sort of man; and he saw the two escaping prisoners, for he came to an abrupt stop.

"How the hell——?" he said.

What happened then was something Singin' Sam McAllister was never able to explain adequately afterward, for the play of events transpired with startling swiftness. That single statement from the lumpish man had identified him as Tate Strunk, and hard on the heels of his words Strunk swept his hand toward his holster, falling sideways as he did so. To Singin' Sam, Tate Strunk was an overzealous prison guard who'd been doing his duty as he saw it, and thus Sam had no desire to swap lead with the man. But circumstances gave him no choice.

Strunk's hand reached his holster, came up with a gun blazing, the bullet plucking at Sam's sleeve. But at that first menacing flutter of Strunk's fingers, McAllister had reached instinctively, snatching at his own gun and firing. Now Strunk joined his hands together across his chest, almost as though he were praying, took two teetering steps forward and fell into a shapeless heap.

"Dead!" Rayburn announced, stepping closer. "He certainly was primed for trouble. Who is he, and what do you suppose made him so edgy?"

McAllister shrugged. "Fogg said there'd be another man coming—a man Alessandro was sending. This is the man, I reckon. And that makes a few things clear that wasn't clear before. But let's get to them cayuses, mister! Those shots will likely bring folks flocking this way!"

Rayburn could understand the wisdom of that suggestion; the two broke into a run toward the horses, picked up the trailing reins and scrambled into saddles. Cutting down the alley behind the jail, they reached the bridge at a high gallop and rumbled over it, the planks thundering beneath them. Rayburn had taken the lead; he pointed his mount to the northeast, and for the first few miles they kept at a hard pace. When they finally paused to rest their heaving horses, they heard no sound of pursuit behind them. Sam said, "Where you heading?"

"The schoolhouse," Rayburn replied. "Perhaps Hope is still thereabouts."

But when they reached the building, it was as dark as Chip had found it the previous night, and the riding of wide circles and the cautious calling of Hope's name brought no results. After a half-hour of this, Rayburn said, "She's just not here. And I don't think she came to town. That would have been too risky, and, besides, if she'd been in Tumble-rock she's have let us know she was there."

"Maybe Chip found her last night," Sam suggested. "But where would he have taken her?"

"To the safest place, likely," Rayburn said. "The one place where she'd be beyond Alessandro's reach. Forlorn Valley."

"Then let's head for the valley," said Singin' Sam. "Chip wants you in Helena, but Chip's still somewhere in these Tumblerocks. I aim to find him."

Thus it was decided, and thus, unwittingly, Clark Rayburn set about doing the very thing that Seton Alessandro had hoped Rayburn would do—return to the valley. The two came along the rim of Bear Creek Basin, and soon they heard faint sounds below them; and Rayburn held up a hand for silence. "Hounds baying!" he said. "And I thought I heard gunshots. What game is Alessandro hunting tonight?"

"Us, likely," Sam decided with a chuckle. "The news of our escape has been fetched to the kingpin. He figgers we're heading for the valley by way of the pass. And he's spreading a net across the basin to hem us in."

"He'll be fooled," Rayburn said. "We're using the stairway to the sky."

They rode along again, Rayburn still leading the way.

They came through the forest of lodgepole pine where the shadows banked blackly, and they were nearly to the valley's rim before the moon rose like a great white moth over the eastern hills. Now Rayburn said, "I've been doing some thinking about tonight. Fogg was on the level all right. He released us and gave us a warning about that fellow Alessandro was sending—the man you shot. But that man had as good a look at one of us as he did at the other. Yet it was you he tried to dust. Why? Because Alessandro knows you're working for the governor?"

"He has another reason, too, for wanting my scalp," Sam admitted. "It's a wild story having to do with an ace of spades and a deal that came off long ago. It doesn't matter, Rayburn."

The Forlorn leader had fallen back to ride stirrup to stirrup beside Singin' Sam. Now Rayburn leaned, his fingers fastening to Sam's arm in a hard and relentless grip. *"An ace of spades!"* Rayburn exclaimed. "What about Alessandro and an ace of spades?"

In this first moonlight, Rayburn's face was like something carved from granite, but his eyes were alive with a fierce, blazing intensity. Singin' Sam said, "Don't break my arm, mister. I'll spin the story for you." Whereupon he told of Ute Kincade, and of Gopher Joe Gravelly who'd died in Deer Lodge, and the story of Grasshopper Gulch and the fabulous poker game Gopher Joe had witnessed. When he'd finished, Rayburn said softly, "I wish I'd known this yesterday. You see, McAllister, I'm the man who sold himself to Alessandro on the turn of a card."

Singin' Sam whistled. "I should have guessed it," he decided at last. "Yet it seemed like everybody in these Tumblerocks was pretty much slave to Alessandro. I'm bettin' you were a professional gambler once. It ain't every man who'd keep a bargain made over a deck of cards. But he gypped you out of twenty years of living!"

"You've turned me free tonight," Rayburn said. "Before the sun rises, I think I shall be calling upon Seton Alessandro."

Something in the way Rayburn said this made Singin' Sam shudder in spite of himself. Sam said, "Alessandro seems to have a long account to settle. But I reckon we'd better get on to the valley—first."

"Yes," Rayburn said like a man speaking in his sleep. "Yes, of course."

They were nearing the top of those switchbacks leading down to the valley's floor, and now it was Singin' Sam who gripped Rayburn's arm. "Rider ahead!" Sam whispered. "See? Swingin' out of a saddle over there by the rim!"

"It's Hope!" Rayburn shouted, and the two went spurring forward.

Hope spied them too and must have recognized the pair, for she came running as Rayburn slipped to the ground. When Rayburn had her in his arms, she cried, "Chip——? He's not with you?"

Rayburn shook his head. "We thought he'd taken you back to the valley. Haven't you seen him?"

"This morning," she said and told how Chip had hunted her down in the darkness of last night, and of his proposal to go to Alessandro's ranch and his assurance that his mission would bring a solution to Clark Rayburn's troubles. Rayburn in turn told his story, but this information, pieced together, netted nothing. A worried frown on his face, Singin' Sam said, "We might as well go down into the valley. Maybe Chip is there; come through the pass. If he isn't, we can start lookin' for him."

So it was agreed, and they urged their mounts down the switchbacks, Rayburn leading the way. The descent was even more breathtaking than the climb had been, but the moon was high enough now to give them light, and Rayburn knew this giant stairway from past experience. Upon the valley's floor, they mounted again, but by then the moon was fading, the night nearly gone. In the dark before the dawn they reached that huddle of log buildings, Forlorn town, and found not a single light showing. But when they racked their weary horses before Rayburn's cabin, a figure detached itself from the shadow of the eaves. "Rayburn?" it cried. "Is that you? Man, I'm glad you've come along!"

Hope thumbed a match aglow and held it cupped in her hands, and Rayburn said, "Ives! Colorado Jack Ives!" His voice turned low and deadly. "So Alessandro has sent his foreman to me. Why, Ives?"

"Easy, now!" Ives snapped. "Can't anybody understand that I'm not Alessandro's man any longer? Chip Halliday sent me here!"

Chip's name was like a steadying hand to Rayburn, and it stiffened Singin' Sam and Hope to tense alertness too. Rayburn said, "Talk, Ives. Talk fast! What do you know about Chip Halliday?"

Whereupon Ives began an accountal, starting with that moment when he'd spied Chip coming toward him down the trail and ending with the episode of their parting in Bear Creek Basin with Alessandro's riders hard on their heels. Understanding grew upon Singin' Sam as Ives talked, and Sam said, "Those hounds, Rayburn! That ruckus we heard down in the basin! It was Chip that Alessandro was hunting, not us!"

"Your sentry let me through the pass," Ives said. "Chip told me to wait for him until noon tomorrow. If he wasn't here by then, I was to lead the Forlorners down upon Alessandro's ranch. But I've gone crazy just hunkering here waiting for the sunrise. I keep remembering him out there alone with Alessandro's crew hemming him in."

"He's in trouble, Ives; no doubt of it," Rayburn said. "And we're bringing him help!"

Drawing his gun, Rayburn blazed at the sky till he'd emptied the forty-five. Before the last echo had died away, lights blossomed in some of the cabins, and a few moments later doors were banging and men spilling out in various stages of dress. Rayburn shouted, "Over here, fellers!" and when the sleepy-eyed men of Forlorn Valley began assembling, staring at him in astonishment, he said, "There's little time for talking. Get saddled up, boys. We've got a war waiting for us on the other side of the pass."

Then there was confusion of getting under way, men hurrying to finish dressing, men throwing gear on saddlers and looking to their guns, and, watching all this, Clark Rayburn smiled at Singin' Sam. "You said that Alessandro gypped me out of twenty years of living," Rayburn observed. "I'm not so sure. He gave me this place as a home. He gave me these people to lead. And this morning the thing he fashioned here in Forlorn Valley is boomeranging on him."

The first flush of dawn was in the east when a score of fighting men headed southward with Clark Rayburn, Singin' Sam McAllister and Colorado Jack Ives at their head. With them rode Hope, in spite of her father's protests. But he had won her promise to stay behind when the shooting started, and he had to be content with that. While they rode, Ives did much talking, telling them of Lia and the danger that threatened her, and Rayburn nodded to this, saying nothing. And so they came winding down the valley, and they passed the scattered herds of Forlorn cattle and began their climb to the top of the pass; and the sun was just beginning to show itself when they approached the boulder where the sentry held sway.

Rayburn said, "Anything stirring this morning, feller?"

The sentry took a look at the full fighting force of the valley arranged at Rayburn's back, swallowed his astonishment and said, "Somebody's hunkering in the brush on down the trail. They ain't showin' themselves, but I know they're there."

"I see," Rayburn said and nudged his horse. When he was a dozen yards beyond the boulder, a gun spat, the lead geysering dirt in the center of the trail. Down below, from a tangle of rocks and brush at one side of the narrowed pass, a voice said, "Nobody's coming out of the valley, mister! Now move back before I raise my sights!"

Rayburn retreated to the shelter of the boulder. "Alessandro's men," he reported. "But there can't be many of them —not with most of the crew busy in the basin."

"He doesn't need many here," McAllister observed. "This valley's always been a safe proposition because one sentry could hold off an army. But that works two ways. A couple of men down below can keep us all penned up in here forever."

"Thunderation, Rayburn!" Colorado Jack protested. "Are

we going to let them stop us? Halliday's out there some-where, and Lia's likely still a prisoner in Alessandro's house. They're both as good as dead unless we can rush this pass!"

"We could go back into the valley and climb the stairway to the sky," Rayburn soliloquized. "But that would be slow going, and it would be nearly noon before we could get this force back around and into Bear Creek Basin. Probably we haven't that much time to waste. But I know a way to sweep this pass clean! The quickest way! Boys, turn back to where that last herd of cattle was grazing. Cut out about a hundred steers and haze them up here mighty fast! We're going to make a battering ram out of beef, and we're going through the pass behind it!"

18 ⋮ Cornered Quarry

Free of Alessandro's ranch, but with the pursuit pounding hard in the twilight, Chip Halliday had watched Colorado Jack Ives ride from sight in the little clump of trees in Bear Creek Basin, watched with a strange sense of loneliness. Ives had gone at Chip's insistence, of course, but for a moment Chip almost regretted this parting of the ways. He had that feeling of impotency that comes to a cowboy afoot, yet his strategy had been sound enough, as he quickly learned. For while he hunkered in the brush, a knot of Alessandro's riders roared by, clinging grimly to the trail of Ives.

Eventually they'd learn that Ives was alone, and when they did some of them would turn back in search of Chip. But meanwhile he had no intention of sitting here waiting for them. With the rataplan of hoofs dying in the distance, Chip was already running to the south again, but he didn't take a straight course. To his far left loomed another clump of trees, and he planned to dodge from shelter to shelter till Alessandro's ranch was far behind him.

But before he reached that second grove, he made out other riders in the dim haze of twilight. They came sweeping from the ranch, a thin, far-flung net that was spread to engulf him, and he ran harder then, scurrying into the timber and plunging on through it to the east, getting this clump of trees between himself and the charging horsemen. Over a rise of ground, he stretched himself flat, and he was this way, his chin pressed tight against the ground, when a rider thundered by, not a dozen yards away.

Chip grinned. More than one could play at this game, and he came to his feet and started south again. But soon he was flinging himself to the earth once more, for another horseman loomed out of the gathering night, almost riding him down. The fellow roared on past, and Chip rose and ran toward the trees, keeping low and straining his eyes for sight of other riders. And that was when he heard the hound pack baying.

At first he didn't recognize the sound, though he remembered hearing it on another night. That had been during the moonlit hours when he and Hope and Singin' Sam had entered this basin on their way to Forlorn Valley, and Hope had spoken then of Alessandro's hunting expeditions and of the hound pack he kept for combing grizzlies out of the Tumblerocks. Now those hounds were on the trail again, and he himself was the quarry. For a moment he fought against a marrow-chilling, primitive panic, for it was one thing to dodge horsemen but quite another to elude the savage brutes that were now hunting him down.

To the east a thin line of willows marked where Bear Creek came tumbling down out of Forlorn Valley to roar southward past Tumblerock town. Throwing caution aside, Chip started on a hard run for the creek. If there was any bloodhound strain in Alessandro's pack, the beasts would be given his scent at the saddle shed where he'd been imprisoned this afternoon, Chip reasoned. But they'd have to do some circling before they picked up his trail again, for he'd left the ranch on horseback.

Reaching the creek, he plunged into it, and, hugging close to the shore, he began bucking the current as he slowly waded upstream. At times the water came to his armpits, and he was certain he was going to be swept off his feet and carried away. Now he could hear no sound of pursuit; there was only the roar of the creek in his ears. He toyed with the thought of heading downstream and decided against it; they'd be keeping careful watch in that direction. When he judged that he'd put many yards behind him, he came to the bank again and lay panting among the willows, chilled and worn.

Somewhere in the distance the hounds were still baying, closer it seemed, and Chip staggered to his feet and lurched aimlessly along. Gone now was any thought of making it to the south; they had him hemmed in and his only hope was to continue to elude them. He crossed an open stretch of ground and got into another clump of trees, but here he almost collided with a man who stood leaning against a tree, resting his horse.

Thick, impenetrable darkness swathed this grove; and it wasn't till Chip heard the man's grunt of surprise that he became aware of the fellow's presence. But there was strength enough left in Chip to send his fist smashing forward. With a throaty roar the man closed with him; the two went down in a writhing tangle of arms and legs, and Chip found himself fighting as he'd never fought before—fighting desperately and with the full knowledge that he must conquer or die.

For Chip had readily sensed why every living thing that looked to Seton Alessandro as its master was being thrown into this search for him. Piute had stood at the corner of the ranch house this afternoon while he, Chip, had listened to Lia Alessandro's tale of the death of St. John. Piute knew what deadly knowledge Chip now possessed, and Piute had doubtless told Seton Alessandro. Alessandro had been expected back at the ranch at any time, and the presence of the hound pack on the trail indicated that Alessandro had indeed returned. Alessandro wanted him dead, for it was Chip's life or Alessandro's now.

Thus Chip fought with all the fury of a cornered grizzly. But this man beneath him was big and burly and hard to overpower. And the fellow was shouting at the top of his lungs, calling for help, giving strident warning that he had the quarry cornered. Getting his hands on the man's throat, Chip squeezed hard, determined to shut off that outcry. But still they went rolling over and over, almost under the legs of the man's cayuse which, range-trained, stood anchored by its own trailing reins.

Like a terrier that had gotten its teeth into a stick, Chip never released his hold on the man's throat. Oblivious to the fellow's battering fists, unmindful of the man's attempts to get his gun unleathered, Chip clung desperately, only dimly aware that the man had long since ceased his shouting and almost unconscious of the fact that the fellow's efforts were growing weaker.

Then the man went limp beneath him. Nearby the horse still towered in the darkness, but now there was a commotion in the timber as men came beating through this clump of trees, frantically shouting. Chip began fumbling at the man's gun-belt, trying to unlatch it, but when it persisted in defying his fingers he groped for the holster and found it empty. The man's gun had fallen out during the fight, which explained why the fellow hadn't been able to bring it into play. Groping feverishly over the ground, Chip found the gun.

He wanted the cartridge belt as well, but there wasn't time. The oncoming men were almost upon him, and he came to a stand and lurched toward the horse. Someone floundered out of the darkness and wrapped an arm around his leg as he swung into the saddle. Turning, Chip clipped at a vague shape with his gun-barrel. This new adversary went down without a groan, and Chip was instantly snatching at the reins, plunging out of the timber.

Now he had a horse beneath him and a gun in his hand, and his spirits soared. Sending two shots behind to discourage those who were closest, he wheeled his horse and drove hard for Bear Creek. Hitting the stream, he forced the mount across and came humping up the eastern bank and out of the willows. Off to the southeast lay the Bear Creek schoolhouse, and he headed toward it at a high gallop. But now the moon was beginning to rise, and by its first light he saw a knot of horsemen between himself and his distant destination.

They'd spied him, too; angry cries were punctuated by spasmodic pistol shots, and Chip wheeled again, heading back for the creek with the breeze in his ears and that shadowy pursuit always behind him. Plunging into the water and reaching the western bank, he saw other riders in the distance, some to the south, some to the west. And he could hear the hound pack baying again. Whichever way he turned there were riders, but he was ready to give them all a run.

He was to spend hours at this—wheeling, dodging, shying from shadows. He saw the moon climb high and tip to the west, and still there was no escape for him. Twice he tried crossing the creek again, and twice he was turned back by bullets. Sometimes he was racing toward the north and Forlorn Valley; sometimes he was trying again to reach the basin's southern end. But always there was someone to bar the way. This was hounds and hare with a vengeance.

Long since Chip had emptied the gun; he had used the bullets sparingly, but there had been times when the pursuit was too close and he'd had no choice but to give them a taste of lead. Thus had he drawn his own fangs, but at least he'd stayed free. Though how long he could keep eluding capture was a question. He saw the strategy of Alessandro's men now; they had formed a gigantic ring without making any real effort at closing it. Yet whenever he approached any part of that ring he was in for a chase, and no matter which direction he headed he found riders awaiting him. The hounds were being kept on leash, he learned, but they were always handy to harry him, to keep him moving.

This was more than a mere cat-and-mouse play. They meant to wear him down; and long before dawn the head of the valiant cayuse he'd commandeered was drooping, and Chip knew his race was about run. Alessandro's men had a chance to rest their mounts; perhaps some had even returned to the ranch for fresh saddlers. But the horse Chip had gotten was lathered and weary, and there weren't many miles left in the mount. Then darkness before dawn settled over the land, and that gave Chip some respite.

They couldn't see him now, they couldn't keep up their constant crowding, and his big concern centered around the hounds who might still hunt him down. He got to the creek again, and he waited in the willows, giving his horse a chance to rest, and in spite of himself he dozed in the saddle. He awoke with a start to find the sun just beginning to rise. Then he was on the move again, but as he came out onto the open floor of the basin, riders spied him and set up a shout.

Instantly Chip was wheeling the horse, heading for the cover of the nearest clump of trees, but now the horse went down, and Chip was kicking his feet free of stirrups for the second time since he'd escaped Alessandro's ranch. Lighting, he turned to step up into the saddle again, and then he realized that it wasn't weariness but a bullet that had brought the horse low. He had taken this horse from one of Alessandro's riders, and he had also taken the unreasoning loyalty a good mount gives to its master, and there were tears of anger in Chip's eyes as he looked at the dying animal. He said, "Damn them! Damn the whole rotten pack of them!"

Three riders came pounding over a rise to roar down upon him. Turning, Chip ran for the willows of the creek, and bullets were pelting about him, clipping leaves from the underbrush as he wormed through it. Reaching the bank, he dived into the creek, letting the current catch him and sweep him downstream. There was little strength left in him to fight against this swift suction, and he only tried to keep his head above the water. He saw the banks go blurring past; his head was buzzing and it took a titanic effort to keep his arms and legs moving.

Perhaps he went unconscious then; the sun was above the eastern hills when he found himself half-sprawled upon the western bank, his legs still in the water; yet he had no remembrance of trying to make it to shore. For a long time he merely lay there, letting the strength seep back into him, and then he stumbled through the underbrush and had his look across the basin floor. It was empty as far as he could see, yet he thought he perceived dim movement far to the north.

Nearer, no more than a mile away, were the buildings of Alessandro's ranch, and it was Chip's wild, jubilant thought that the current of Bear Creek had swept him beyond that ring of riders and to comparative safety. Something flashed in the distance, to the north, something that might have been sunlight upon a mirror, and he saw another flash to the far west. That made no sense, and he was too tired to try puzzling out the cause of those sun flashes. He went stalking toward Alessandro's ranch, for if his theory was correct and he'd broken through the ring of riders, he might steal a horse before the crew moved southward combing the country for him.

Such was his plan, and he came from one clump of trees to another, lurching out of the last one almost a stone's throw to the rear of the big barn. Careful scrutiny had revealed no signs of humans around the ranch. But adjacent to the barn were the corrals, and he'd spied saddlers in them. He was also aware that he could be seen from the upper rear windows of the ranch house, but he adopted boldness as his strategy and went stalking swiftly toward the corrals. And that was when Seton Alessandro stepped out of the barn and came striding to a stand near the corrals, barring his way.

He came so suddenly that he might have been something

conjured up out of the weariness of Chip's brain. He stood spread-legged in the open space between the corrals and the barn. He had an express rifle under his arm, and he put the stock against his hip while his finger curled around the trigger, and he said, "Hello, Halliday."

That brought Chip to an abrupt stop. He shook his head and knew then that Alessandro was no blurry figment but grim reality, and he said wonderingly, "How did you get here?"

"My boys have had their eyes on you for quite a while," Alessandro said. "They're spread out to the north, and they're now closing in. Hear the hounds baying? And did you see those sun flashes a while ago? Sun talk, Halliday. Heliographs—a device used by the British Army in the hill country of Northern India. It also makes a very adequate signaling system here in the Tumblerocks. Those sun flashes told me you'd been sighted and were heading this way. I've had only to wait."

"And now——?" Chip said.

"And now the hunt is over, the quarry cornered. Another little adaptation of the Indian system. I had merely to sit here waiting; my men have flushed my game to me. And it's almost with regret that I shall bring you down, Halliday. You've made game worthy of the huntsman. But now I must give you your choice. Do you prefer to turn and run toward my men who are even now pouring out of yonder clump of trees? Or shall I have the honor of rendering the *coup de grace*?"

This was the finish. Behind him Chip could hear the rising thunder of hooves, the throaty baying of hounds unleashed. Before him Alessandro smiled and bided his time. But there was within Chip one last need, and that was to go down fighting. "To hell with you!" he said and lurched blindly forward to where Alessandro stood waiting.

19 : Drink to the Devil!

Jasper Fogg found himself on the floor of his office when the new day grayed the window. How he came to be here, when he'd returned, he didn't know; his clothes were rumpled and stained, his muscles ached from the hard bedding the bare planks had provided, his head was clamorous and his mouth tasted foul. Also he was cold, for the chill of the morning was in this room. Somewhere a rooster was cock-a-doodling the dawn; a pump creaked rustily and a shutter was banging open on a nearby building. These familiar sounds of Tumblerock's awakening had also awakened him.

Coming to an awkward stand, he surveyed the wreckage of his baggy black suit and thought for a moment he was going to be sick. Pushing his hand through his unkempt gray hair, he leaned against his desk, and it was then he saw the note Seton Alessandro had left for him the previous afternoon. He read it, finding it an imperious command to put in an appearance at Alessandro's ranch as quickly as possible. Balling the paper in his fist, he hurled it away.

"Jump!" he mumbled. "Jump when he cracks the whip! Play you're a little circus dog and go through the paper hoop when the master wishes it!"

But memories of the preceding day and night were beginning to come back to him, and he pieced them together only
to find many gaps remaining. There'd been the coroner's
inquest and that session with Alessandro in this very office.
Tate Strunk . . . ? Yes, Strunk had come and Alessandro
had given the man an assignment which was to cost the life
of Singin' Sam McAllister and shatter the chances of Clark
Rayburn or any other Forlorner to ever stand a free man. It
was that little deal that had sent Fogg out to seek the solace
of the bottle. Blazes, a man couldn't stomach everything!

He'd visited quite a few saloons yesterday afternoon and
evening, had Jasper Fogg. He tried to place them in their
proper sequence, but once again there were gaps. But now
he was remembering an interlude in that parade of drinking
places—an interlude that had taken him to the livery stable
where finding the hostler gone, he'd helped himself to a pair
of saddle horses. Saddle horses! He'd taken them to the jail
building, and he'd searched Frank Busby's deserted office
for keys. And given those same keys to Clark Rayburn!

It was all coming back to him now, and the significance of
the thing he'd done, striking him at this comparatively sober
moment, sent him searching for that note of Alessandro's
again. Alessandro knew! That was it! And Alessandro was
sending for him in order to mete out punishment!

A wild, unreasonable fear gripping him, Fogg reread the
note. Nothing there to tell a man what had prompted Alessandro to write it. Slowly logic began to assert itself; a fine
brain had belonged to Jasper Fogg before the maggots of
alcohol had begun crawling within it. Alessandro had been
here in the office when Fogg had last seen him. Possibly
Alessandro had wanted to discuss the coming trial of Clark
Rayburn, for Fogg would be given an all-important role at
that trial. Alessandro had waited for Fogg's return, and
when Fogg had failed to show himself Alessandro had left
that note, ordering him to the ranch.

That was it. There was no way Seton Alessandro or any

other man could guess that it had been Jasper Fogg who'd released Rayburn and Singin' Sam from the jail. Yet the fear was still in his stomach.

Lurching out of the office, Fogg crossed over to a café. The place had just opened for the day; dishes clattered noisily in the kitchen, and Fogg perched himself upon a stool and ordered coffee. The steaming brew quieted his stomach and did something for his nerves as well, and he eyed the cook casually and said, "Seton Alessandro around town?"

"Not since late yesterday afternoon," the man said. "I saw him head out in the direction of his ranch."

"Thanks. I'll be riding that way."

Comforted by what he'd learned, Fogg went to the livery stable, got the gentle-gaited mount he sometimes rented, and set forth for the ranch. If Alessandro had left before dark yesterday, then Alessandro couldn't have had the escape of Rayburn and McAllister on his mind when he'd penned that note. And so the lawyer rode along with renewed assurance, the fresh air clearing his head as he crossed the dew-bejeweled range.

By the time he'd sighted Alessandro's buildings, he was wishing he'd gotten a pint of whisky at one of the saloons before leaving town. He needed the hair of the dog that had bitten him, and he assured himself that just a bracer would turn the trick. But likely it was best that he had no bottle. Alessandro would be in a fine frenzy over that spree of yesterday, and Alessandro's anger would be the greater if there was any sign that Jasper Fogg had gotten himself a good start on a second drunk.

"Got to get his royal permission to even wet my whistle," Fogg muttered aloud. "Got to live the way he wants me to live, think the thoughts he puts in my head, do the sneaking things he wants done."

Angry with the impotent anger of a sick and troubled man, he reached the ranch to find it silent and deserted. But as he dismounted at the front gate, the door of the house creaked open and he was confronted by a leveled gun in the hand of one of Alessandro's crew. This was Yampa, and the sentry said, "Oh, it's you." Dropping his iron back into leather, he added, "Alessandro said you might be along. The whole bunch has gone riding, but they'll likely be back soon. The boss said for you to wait in his study for him. Here's the key."

Lurching inside and fumbling at the door of the study, Fogg said, "Got any coffee on the fire?"

Yampa shook his head, and Fogg said, "Then make some, damn it!" He had noted the contemptuous way that Yampa had dumped his gun back into its holster upon recognizing him, and something about the gesture had been oddly irritating to Fogg.

"Alessandro's got his girl locked upstairs," Yampa said. "You know that. My orders are to stay up there and make sure she keeps to her room."

"She can't gnaw her way through a locked door," Fogg snapped. "I'll run upstairs and do the waiting while you get that coffee brewing."

Turning his back on Yampa, he lumbered up the stairs and came along the second story hallway to the one door that was closed. "You in there, Lia?" he asked.

Something rustled beyond the door. "Mr. Fogg——? Is that you? Where's Yampa?"

"Making coffee," Fogg said. "I'll see that you get a cup if you want it, girl. And some breakfast too."

"You can do more than that for me, Mr. Fogg," she said. "Let me out of here!"

He saw the key hanging on the nail by the door, but he said, "I can't do that, Lia. You know I can't."

She said, "Please, Mr. Fogg! And hurry before Yampa comes back! You want to help me—I know you do. I watched your face the other night when *he* brought Jack and me down to his study. You hated him as much as I did when he was humiliating me. And he's going to kill me, Fogg. I could see it in his eyes when I shouted Justin St. John's name at him. Please let me out of here while there's still time!"

He lifted his hand toward the key. All the decency that was left in him prompted that gesture. He wanted to help her, just as he'd wanted to help Clark Rayburn at that trumped-up inquest. And already he'd taken cards against Alessandro. He'd defied the man when he'd released Rayburn and McAllister from the jail, and he was remembering that he'd gloried in that defiance at the time. But that little coup had been carefully, if drunkenly planned. There'd been no real risk attendant to it, and little chance that his part would ever be revealed. But releasing Lia Alessandro would be a different matter. There was Yampa downstairs, but it was the thought of Seton Alessandro that really dropped Fogg's hand to his side.

"I can't do it," he muttered, and went stumbling away from the door.

He heard her cry after him, but he shut his ears and his heart to the plea. He went to the foot of the stairs, and here he waited until Yampa appeared from the rear of the house. "Coffee's ready in the kitchen," Yampa said sullenly. "It's as good as I could make it. The cook's off with the rest of the crew."

"See if Miss Alessandro wants some," Fogg said.

Drinking the coffee, Fogg wondered what need had taken even the cook away on some sort of pasear. He came to the study then, admitting himself and shooting up the blinds to let in the morning sunlight. And he eyed the wine decanter on Alessandro's desk, and took it into his hand to pour himself a drink.

Ah, but this heathenish stuff was no good for a whisky-drinking man. He set the decanter down and began an aimless prowling of the room, a more troubled man now than he'd been when he'd ridden here; but there was no turning his back on this thing that now beset him. It was Lia's plea, and it still rang in his ears; and the feeling grew upon him that he would hear her voice until his dying day.

For Lia was doomed, and Jasper Fogg knew it. His knowledge was part of that vast and forbidden store of knowledge he'd accumulated concerning Seton Alessandro. What was it the man had said to him in this very room? ". . . I've told you too much about myself, Fogg. Far, far too much . . ." Aye, Lia was doomed. If Seton Alessandro loved anything in this world, he loved Lia. But greater than that love was Alessandro's concern for his own skin. And that was why Lia was going to die.

And now it came to Jasper Fogg that Lia's blood would also be on his hands. He had his chance to free Lia, and he was throwing away that chance; and that made him guilty, too. A man could rationalize his every act; a man could drink himself into sodden forgetfulness, but there were some things he could never escape. One bold act of betrayal, and Lia might be free. One show of courage and the trick would be turned.

He wasn't conscious of making a decision, but he found himself rummaging through Alessandro's desk. He had Yampa to remove before he could reach that upstairs room, and he wanted the fancy silver-inlaid forty-five that Alessandro kept in his desk. But the gun was gone now, he discovered; the only familiar object Fogg found was that faded tintype of a dark and exotic woman's face. This he pocketed, and then he turned to the gun case that stood against one wall.

Here were guns a-plenty, ancient guns and modern guns, and many of them were loaded. But the case was locked, and Alessandro doubtless carried the key. Like a man mesmerized, Fogg strode to the fireplace, picked up a poker and proceeded to smash out the glass. He was selecting a loaded revolver for himself when Yampa's boots beat warningly against the stairs. The noise was fetching the man! Instantly

Fogg was lurching to the doorway, and he stood poised to one side of it as Yampa thrust his head into the room.

"What in thunder——" Yampa started to say as he saw the havoc that had been wrought. But Fogg's smashing gun-barrel broke off Yampa's speech abruptly, sending the man pitching face forward to lie crumpled upon the floor.

For an instant Fogg stood looking down upon the fallen man, and he realized then that he'd struck too hard and Yampa was dead. Likewise he knew that the die was cast and that he, himself, was doomed. Alessandro had been expecting Jasper Fogg, and Alessandro would therefore guess who'd done this thing. And there was that cook in the café in Tumblerock this morning. Fogg had told the man that his trail was taking him to this ranch. Thus the web had been woven, and Jasper Fogg was hopelessly entangled within it.

But he had struck his first telling blow at Seton Alessandro when he'd wielded that gun-barrel, and the thought, strangely, brought him not consternation but a feeling of elation that squared his shoulders and gave him stature. He was about to step through the doorway when an impulse seized him—a queer whim of a man who'd made dramatics a part of his profession. Sloshing a glass full of wine from the decanter, he hoisted the drink and then kicked at the teak-wood desk, sending it crashing over.

"Here's to you, Alessandro," he said aloud. "Here's a drink to you, you sneaking, scheming, heartless devil. Here's to the noose I'll put around your neck!"

He downed the wine, gagged at the taste of it, stepped over Yampa's sprawled body and started up the stairs. And somewhere in that ascent he felt the first tremor run through him. Gritting his teeth, his muscles tensed again and a chill struck him though perspiration beaded his forehead. And because the twitching of his body would not cease when he willed it to, he suddenly understood, for he'd read about such symptoms somewhere.

"Strychnine!" he groaned aloud. *"The devil put strychnine in the wine!"*

Of all the terrors he had known, this terror that was devastating him now was the greatest. He reached the top of the stairs, but a convulsion seized him and he writhed upon the floor, fighting against it. Dimly he knew that his need was for an emetic of some kind, and he thought of the kitchen below. But he also knew that he would never have the strength to climb these stairs a second time, and Lia was still locked in yonder room.

That made a hard choice for him, but his hatred of Alessandro forced the decision. He could see it all now. That note fetching him out here. That key to a locked study—the key Yampa had been instructed to turn over to him! Those things had been part of a carefully laid plan to kill him. Why Alessandro wanted him dead, he didn't know. But he knew that Alessandro had been sure that Jasper Fogg, left alone in the study, would be tempted by the wine decanter that was left waiting with death in it.

And thus, in the midst of his agony, Fogg's one compelling thought was still to thwart Alessandro, at least in part. He got to Lia's door, hauled himself upward by clutching at the knob, and he fumbled the key into the lock, turned it, and sprawled inside the room.

Sweat was in his eyes, and he could hardly see the horrified girl. She stood over by the window, her eyes wide, and he wondered if she understood how near to death he was, or if she merely presumed he was drunk again. She was shouting something, and her words pierced through his agony and reached him. She was saying, *"Alessandro! Out there by the corrals! He's raising his gun to kill Chip Halliday!"*

A new paroxysm was seizing Fogg, but he crawled to the window, got his hands on the sill and smashed out the glass with his gun-barrel. Perspiration blinded him; he swept it away with a toss of his head, and he saw Alessandro out yonder, and another man facing him, and, in the distance sweeping out of a clump of trees to the north, the full force of Alessandro's crew.

All this Fogg saw, and then he had his sights lined on Alessandro. But the whole world was wavering, and he had to muster the last of his strength to hold steady on his target. *"Alessandro!"* he shouted, but it seemed no more than a feeble croak.

Yet his voice brought Alessandro half turning around, and that was when Fogg squeezed the trigger. For Jasper Fogg, facing the tribunal of his own conscience for the last time, was rendering justice unto himself and unto Seton Alessandro. The thunder of the gun filled the room, and out yonder Alessandro was flinging up his arms, his knees buckling beneath him. And with that picture to carry with him into eternity, Jasper Fogg slid gently to the floor.

20 : Page from the Past

Chip had covered half the distance between himself and Alessandro, covered it with the certainty that he was charging to his death, when he saw Alessandro swing his head as that faint, croaking call came from the house. There was time for Alessandro to take that look and still cut Chip down. But then a gun blasted, and Alessandro was tossing his rifle away and coming down to his knees, his face contorted with pain and anger and fear. For a space he seemed to hold to life through sheer will, and then he had the look of a man who was making a losing fight and knew it; and with that look upon him he died.

But others as well as Chip had witnessed his passing; there was a wild shout from those riders who were sweeping down out of the basin, and that cry snapped Chip from his stunned contemplation of Alessandro's body. The riders, led by Piute, would soon be upon him; already the guns were speaking, and Chip lunged forward and snatched up the rifle that had fallen from Alessandro's fingers.

He got the gun, and he put it into action as he spun about. Triggering twice, he ran for the nearest corral, swarmed to its top pole and stationed himself there. He lined a target in his sights, squeezed the trigger, and Piute threw up his arms in a jerky, futile gesture and pitched out of his saddle. Another man fell, and another, and the fury of the charge was broken as the riders of Alessandro wheeled their mounts in hasty retreat. The hounds unleashed, milled in confusion.

The riders would be charging again, Chip knew. They were panicked for the moment; they'd seen Alessandro go down, and they'd seen their foreman die, and that had taken some of the fight out of them, but they still had to have the scalp of Chip Halliday, who could bring them all to trial. Thus Chip sensed that the end had merely been postponed for him, but he had a gun in his hand and that made a difference. The hunted had turned hunter; and he sent a shot at the retreating riders to show them his present temper.

Coming down from the corral, he started backing toward the house to make his stand. But before he reached shelter, Alessandro's riders had turned again, were galloping down upon him, but now Chip's eyes widened for something else was pouring out of that clump of trees that shut off a broader view of the basin's northward sweep. Cattle! Scores of stampeding cattle! Racketing guns had smothered the sound of those pounding hooves, but a herd was here. And with it were riders who hazed the steers along, shouting and snapping rope ends and firing as they came.

That man to the far left—that tall, blond man! Clark Rayburn! And Singin' Sam was in a saddle, and Colorado Jack, and many others! They were upon Alessandro's bewildered riders in a churning maelstrom of steers and horses, yapping hounds and cursing men, and there was no need now for Chip to finish his fighting.

The melee spilled down upon the ranch, engulfing the buildings, battered up against the corrals. Dust and powder-smoke put a haze in the air, and shouts and curses roared above the rattling of hooves, the squeal of saddle leather, the banging of guns. Backed against the enclosure that had held the hounds, Chip saw a rider plow to a stop beside him and swing from a saddle; and suddenly Hope was in his arms.

"Chip, you're safe!" she cried and began sobbing.

"Both feet on the ground, darling," he said, stroking her hair.

Clark Rayburn joined them a moment later, and Singin' Sam McAllister, and when the four came around to the front of the house they found Colorado Jack Ives already fumbling at the door. "Upstairs," Chip said. "Somebody shot Alessandro from one of the rear windows. And saved my life."

Into the hallway, they had a glimpse of the study, seeing the overturned desk and the smashed gun case and the sprawled body of Yampa. Then they were crowding up the steps and into the open doorway of Lia's room, and here Jasper Fogg lay upon the floor, his head cradled in Lia's lap. The girl lifted tear-dimmed eyes to them, and she said, "He is dead. I tried to help him, but there was nothing I could do. It was he who killed Alessandro."

Ives's fists clenched spasmodically, then unclenched. "Alessandro—dead!" he said. "Once I thought that if there was any justice under heaven, it would be me who'd put a bullet into Alessandro. But perhaps this was as it should have been. He used us all for pawns, but he brought the greatest ruin to Fogg. The rest of us he couldn't wreck completely, but he tore down Fogg as a great building is torn down, brick by brick, until there was nothing left but a shell. Yes, Fogg had the real score to settle. I'm glad he got his chance to do it."

Clark Rayburn's face softened, too. "You're right, Ives," he said. "I wanted Alessandro's life more than you did. But in the end, the account is closed. I know now that Alessandro never took anything from me, really."

Colorado Jack drew Lia to her feet and held her close. From the window Chip glanced down into the yard below, and he saw the remnants of Alessandro's riders lined against the barn, their hands lifted high while Forlorn men kept them under steady guns. He said, "The fight seems to be over. Sam, our work in the Tumblerocks is done. Rayburn, you're a free man, it was Alessandro who killed Justin St. John, and I can prove it. It makes a long story, and the telling can wait till later. But the law has no claim on you."

Over Lia's head, Ives said, "Halliday, there's an old rustling charge against me down in the Powder River country. It sent me heading for Forlorn Valley years ago. But I stopped at Seton Alessandro's door on the way, and he made me a proposition to work for him. That was the beginning. But do you suppose that blanket pardon of the governor's covers me, too?"

Chip smiled. "We made a pair of partners yesterday, Ives," he said. "Whatever you did in the past, I reckon you've earned a pardon twice over. And if that paper I packed doesn't cover you, we'll get a special one that will. Sam or me could likely talk the governor out of the shirt off his back right now."

Ives said, "Do you hear that, Lia? I've got a clean name to give you."

She said, "But I've no name at all! Was Alessandro telling the truth the other night when he spoke of India? Look at this, Jack; it's a tintype that fell out of Fogg's pocket as he writhed upon the floor. It's a picture of me, Jack—only it isn't. How do you suppose Fogg came to have it? Perhaps it would have been better if he or Alessandro had lived to answer for this picture."

She revealed the tintype which she'd held clutched in her hand, and Rayburn took it from her, almost reverently, and cupped it in his own hand. "I can answer for this picture," he said. "It is of Donna Conchita y Brenandano, most beautiful of a family that was famed for the beauty of its women and the handsomeness of its men. Pure Castillian she was, and the toast of Mexico City a score of years and more ago."

"Alessandro's wife?" Chip asked, peering over Rayburn's shoulder.

"No, she was a distant cousin of Alessandro's though," Rayburn said. "He was only part Spanish, you know. Friends, this woman was *my* wife. Your mother, Hope; and yours, too, Lia. You see, you girls are sisters."

"Things," opined Singin' Sam McAllister, "are crowdin' a mite too fast for me!"

Night had come again to Tumblerock, and six people were gathered in the study of Seton Alessandro's town house. This was Lia's house now; an examination of Jasper Fogg's office had revealed a will whereby Alessandro had bequeathed his entire holdings to the girl who'd borne his name. And thus Chip Halliday, Singin' Sam McAllister, Colorado Jack Ives, Hope and Clark Rayburn sat now as Lia's guests.

They had much to talk about, this group; they had pieced together their separate experiences of the last few days, and from the fragments they had constructed a coherent whole. Thus Chip had learned, among other things, how the Forlorners had hazed a hundred steers up into the pass and sent them stampeding through, sweeping Alessandro's posted men before them. Those same steers had been urged on southward at a hard run, and there'd been no man to bar the way, for Alessandro's crew had been closing in on the ranch and the quarry they'd cornered. And thus had the Forlorners been in on the fighting finish.

Below this house, down along the main street of the town, those same Forlorners filled the saloons, the men of the valley celebrating the freedom that had been bestowed upon them by Rayburn's formal announcement of the governor's pardon a few hours before. Rumor had it that Sheriff Frank

Busby and his deputies had lined out of town earlier, and the betting ran that the lawmen who'd played Alessandro's game would never show themselves in the Tumblerocks again. The jail was filled to bursting with Alessandro's captured crew, and Singin' Sam had elected himself temporary sheriff.

"Ain't a man in the Tumblerocks knows more about the inside of that calaboose than me," he'd declared when stating his qualifications.

But now there was one last tale to be told, a page from Clark Rayburn's past, and the others had waited patiently for the telling. An old wine had mellowed Rayburn, a new contentment had taken the shadows from his eyes, and he smiled upon his two daughters who were seated side by side on a divan, the one so blond, the other dark and exotic.

"I met your mother in Mexico City, some twenty-five years ago," he said. "I was a professional gambler then, a man who'd done a lot of roving. But I knew I'd found what I'd been seeking when I saw her, and I began courting her at once. I had rivals, of course—many of them—and one was Seton Alessandro, whose relationship to the Brenandanos was very distant.

"Your mother chose me. Don't ask me why; I'll always marvel that she married a gringo gambler who had nothing to offer her but promises when she might have had the pick of the world. We came to the States afterward, and at last to Grasshopper Gulch where there was news of a gold strike. By then the two of you had been born; you first, Hope, and Lia two years later."

"And Alessandro was in Grasshopper Gulch," Singin' Sam interjected, remembering the tale Gopher Joe Gravelly had told Ute Kincade.

Rayburn nodded. "Sometimes I think he knew every move we made and followed us. He still loved Donna, I know, and he was never the kind to give up when he desired something. But Donna died in Grasshopper Gulch the first winter, and

I'd have been willing to die too, except that I had you girls to raise. And the irony of it was that I was rich—rich enough to have given your mother everything. My claim in the gulch had paid off as well as Alessandro's, which was one of the best."

"And you got into that card game then?" Chip asked.

"That was part of Alessandro's scheming; I can see it now," Rayburn said. "Donna was gone, but he hated me the more because his chance of taking her from me was gone too. He wanted me ruined, and he ruined me in that game, stripping me of everything I owned. That's what made me desperate. I had my girls to raise, and I'd let everything I possessed cross that table. So I made that one last deal—the deal whereby I staked myself against what I'd lost. And lost again on the turn of a crooked card, though I didn't know that till last night."

"And you never welshed on a deal like that!" Ives marveled.

Rayburn shook his head. "I'd been a professional gambler, and that made it a matter of honor. Alessandro was likely taking that into account. But he insisted that I turn Lia over to him; she was to be his hostage, his assurance that I'd keep the bargain I'd made. He had another reason, of course. Hope was my girl, blond and blue-eyed, but Lia was her mother all over again. The love that Seton Alessandro had lost had been transferred to the image of Donna Brenandano. And so Lia went to live with him, and Hope went to an academy in Helena, where I registered her under the Anglicized version of her mother's maiden name.

"Alessandro had come to Tumblerock by then, bringing his gold from Grasshopper Gulch. And here he found out about the outlaw sanctuary of Forlorn Valley to the north, and saw the possibility of making himself richer by acting as middleman for the valley. I was installed in the valley to see that the Forlorners never resented his fat pickings too highly. And thus he had the perfect setup. There was Jasper Fogg under his thumb to handle any shady legal dealings for him, Colorado Jack, here, equally his slave, and able to take care of his ranch, and me to handle the valley. It left Alessandro free to roam the world at will."

"But if you'd only told me the truth!" Lia cried.

Rayburn's eyes clouded. "When you were old enough to understand, it was too late. I'd lost you to him; or so I thought. He'd made you love him, and he loved you, too, in his own queer way, though that wouldn't have kept him from putting a bullet in you if you jeopardized his neck with your knowledge of what had happened to St. John. And for the sake of both you girls, my hands were tied. He was seeing that you got schooling and adequate care. That was more than I could have given you if I'd broken my pledge to him and taken you for myself."

He glanced at Hope. "That's why I tried to send you away when you came to the Tumblerocks and hunted me down. I couldn't deny our relationship, but I could offer you nothing —not even a home. The valley was a prison—then. Yet it did something to me to have you here, Hope—stirred up all the growing dissatisfaction of the years. I'd lost one daughter to Alessandro, but I had another. That's why I began to kick over the traces, begging Alessandro to release me from our old bargain and to let me leave this range and take you with me. And that's when he began scheming against me once more. When I'd outlived my usefulness, I was to be destroyed. I'm convinced that it was more than chance that sent Alessandro to Bear Creek Schoolhouse with St. John's body on the very night I was there. Probably he saw the note that one of his bullwhackers fetched me from you, Hope— the note that brought me to the schoolhouse that particular night."

He spread his hands in a simple gesture. "That's all there is to tell," he said.

Lia crossed over to him and laid her hand on his shoulder. "I think I understand," she said softly. "The best that could be had for both of us girls; that is what you wanted. The fortune that Alessandro won on a crooked card will be yours again; I'll see to that. And Jack and I shall be running the basin ranch. We'll always be near you, to make up for the years that were lost."

Rayburn took her hand. "I'll have land in the valley," he said. "All these years I've waited to be free of Forlorn, and now I know I'll never be happy anywhere else. That's part of the reason why I said this morning that Alessandro never took anything from me, really."

Hope crossed over to her father and sister, and Chip chose that moment to slip quietly from the room. Out upon the wide porch, he stood looking down upon the lights of Tumblerock town; and the door behind him opened and closed. That was Singin' Sam, he supposed, removing himself from the family reunion, but Chip didn't turn to look. Not until the door opened and closed once more, and he felt Hope's fingers upon his arm. She said softly, "And you, Chip——?"

"That depends," he said. "You wanted a man with both feet on the ground. I've told you about last night, Hope—how they hunted me across the basin like some wild beast. It made me do some thinking—about living and dying. And it made me want to live very much, to live quietly and peacefully, the way folks are supposed to live. But maybe the change came over me before that—maybe it started that first night when I woke up in the Bear Creek teacherage."

She said, "It doesn't much matter to me how you want to live, Chip. So long as I figure into the scheme somehow."

He drew in his breath sharply, and took her into his arms and held her close. "I've got it all planned," he said. "There's land for the asking in Forlorn and cattle on Iron Hat Halliday's spread that wear my own brand. It will give us a fine start, girl, and it will mean that we'll all be close together—you and I and your dad and Lia and Jack. Maybe even Singin' Sam."

Over in the shadows that cloaked the far end of the porch, Singin' Sam coughed, blew his nose vigorously, and started striding down the hill. . . .

No teetotaler, Singin' Sam McAllister was as wont to take a drink as the next man, but only when the work was done. He had come to the Tumblerocks with a mission to fulfill, and today had seen its completion. Accordingly, he made the rounds of the Tumblerock saloons, and there were celebrating Forlorners to hail him as a hero and buy the drinks for him, and he had wetted his luxuriant yellow moustache many times before an hour ran out.

But still there were a few last odds and ends to take care of, though the thought of them didn't trouble him greatly as he contemplated himself in a series of bar mirrors. But there was a heap of stolen horses to be reshuffled in these here Tumblerocks, he recalled. Him and Chip had certainly been handy with other people's cayuses, and they'd even left a stolen freight wagon on the back trail. He wondered if the governor might after all have to issue another pardon to cover the activities of himself and Chip on this trouble-shooting job.

He had a drink on the governor, and one on the house, then shaking himself free of the happy Forlorners, he wended his erratic way to the telegraph office. Here he drew a yellow form before him, addressed it to the governor of Montana, and penciled the following:

TURN LOOSE YOUR SETTLERS GOVERNOR STOP FORLORN VALLEY IS WIDE OPEN AND FEELING ITS OATS STOP DETAILED REPORT FOLLOWING BUT NOT TOO SOON STOP NEVER WAS NO HAND AT LETTER WRITING.

"Send 'er collect," he ordered the astonished telegrapher who counted the words. "And wait! Got another one for you."

The second blank, addressed to Iron Hat Halliday, read:

TOLD YOU I'D RAISE THAT KID OF YOURN PROPER IF I WAS GIVEN ENOUGH TIME STOP HAPPY TO REPORT THAT CHIP IS ROPED, HOG-TIED AND READY FOR THE BRANDING IRON STOP BETTER GET YOUR TOWN SUIT OUT OF MOTHBALLS AND SLOPE OVER HERE FOR THE WEDDING.

Studying his effort, Sam wetted the pencil and added a postscript:

PS. AND BRING ALONG SOME COWS STOP ME AND CHIP IS STARTING US A RANCH IN FOR-LORN VALLEY AND I'M FOREMAN STOP RESIGNATION TO YOU FOLLOWING BY MAIL STOP BUT NOT TOO DAMNED SOON.

"Send that un collect too," Sam said and burst into song as he left the office:

> Oh once in the saddle, I used to go dashin',
> Oh once in the saddle, I used to be gay,
> Got mixed up with drinkin' an' took to card
>   playin',
> Got shot through the belly; I'm dyin'
>   to-da-a-a-y . . .

And so he went lurching down the street, weaving his unsteady way, and only those who knew him best could have gauged the high and happy state of his spirits by the sad and mournful song that poured from him. . . .

J.T. EDSON

Brings to Life the Fierce and Often Bloody Struggles of the Untamed West

_THE BAD BUNCH	20764-9	$3.50
_THE FASTEST GUN IN TEXAS	20818-1	$3.50
_NO FINGER ON THE TRIGGER	20749-5	$3.50
_ALVIN FOG, TEXAS RANGER	21034-8	$3.50
_HELL IN PALO DURO	21037-2	$3.99
_OLE DEVIL AND THE MULE TRAIN	21036-4	$3.50
_VIRIDIAN'S TRAIL	21039-9	$3.99
_OLE DEVIL AND THE CAPLOCKS	21042-9	$3.99
_TO ARMS! TO ARMS IN DIXIE!	21043-7	$3.99
_TEXAS FURY	21044-5	$3.99

FLOATING OUTFIT SERIES

_GO BACK TO HELL	21033-X	$3.50